HEARTSIDE BAY

THE HEARTSIDE BAY SERIES

1. The New Girl
2. The Trouble With Love
3. More Than a Love Song
4. A Date With Fate
5. Never a Perfect Moment
6. Kiss at Midnight
7. Back to You
8. Summer of Secrets
9. Playing the Game
10. Flirting With Danger
11. Lovers and Losers
12. Winter Wonderland

HEARTSIDE BAY

Playing the Game

CATHY COLE

SCHOLASTIC

Scholastic Children's Books
An imprint of Scholastic Ltd
Euston House, 24 Eversholt Street, London, NW1 1DB, UK
Registered office: Westfield Road, Southam, Warwickshire, CV47 0RA

First published in the UK by Scholastic Ltd, 2014

ISBN 978 1407 14300 2

A CIP catalogue record for this book
is available from the British Library.

Printed by CPI Group (UK) Ltd, Croydon, CR0 4YY
Papers used by Scholastic Children's Books are made
from wood grown in sustainable forests.

1 3 5 7 9 10 8 6 4 2

www.scholastic.co.uk

A bucketful of thanks to
Lucy Courtenay and Sara Grant

ONE

The Heartbeat Café had seen a lot of parties lately, but this one was the biggest Lila could remember. She adjusted her black silk dress and wished she hadn't drunk her mocktail as quickly as she had. It had been delicious, but now she just felt awkward standing by the stage with an empty glass in her hand.

Scientists and deep-sea divers, ballerinas and plumbers, DJs and professors were still flooding in through the doors, their tickets clutched in their hands and their eyes wide as they took in the packed space and the decorations. The whole school had been buzzing with stories about Eve Somerstown's latest party for days. Now that term was finally over and the summer holidays were here, it was clear that every teenager in Heartside Bay wanted a part of the action. Lila envied their imaginative costumes and adjusted her plain black dress again.

Speakers hung on the café's panelled walls had been pouring out music for the past half an hour. As she listened, Lila had to laugh. She leaned a little closer to Josh.

"Have you noticed the songs? Every single one has had the word 'future' in the lyrics!"

"Eve's hardly going to just put her music library on shuffle," Josh shouted back, and kissed the tip of Lila's ear. "She's not the party queen of Heartside Bay for nothing."

As part of the evening's entertainment, Eve had booked Josh to do drawings of people in their outfits from eight o'clock onwards on special WHO DO YOU WANT TO BE? headed cards printed for the party. Lila and Josh had arrived early so Josh could set up his caricature stand by the stage.

"Make sure you dress like your future artistic self," Eve had instructed Josh earlier in the week, surrounded by to-do lists in multiple colours. "A paint-splattered smock would be good."

Josh had looked appalled. "I was thinking more T-shirt and jeans," he said. "I'm going to be an illustrator and graphic novelist, not Vincent van Gogh."

"A smock would be perfect, Josh," Eve had coaxed. "And maybe a beret. This is a party about *future careers*. No one wants to see you dressed as an ordinary person."

Josh could be just as stubborn as Eve when he wanted to be. "It's T-shirt and jeans or nothing, Eve," he said as Lila giggled at the thought of her boyfriend in a smock and a hat.

Wisely, Eve had given up that particular fight. Josh wasn't the dressing-up type. The only concession he'd made to Eve's fancy-dress theme was a coloured pencil he'd stuck behind his ear. He'd bought a set of them for the summer illustration course he was starting on Monday.

Even that's more imaginative than my outfit, Lila thought to herself with a sigh. *How am I supposed to dress up as something I haven't decided on yet?*

She glanced around the room, trying to pick out her friends in the crowd. Eve was easy to spot, directing troops by the bar in a close-fitting green dress. A shiny silver crown with the words PARTY PLANNER TO THE STARS written around the brim was sitting on her sleekly pulled back auburn hair. She was organizing trays of drinks for the waiters in their WHAT DO YOU WANT TO BE? T-shirts to offer the guests as the came through the doors. Eve's girlfriend Becca stood beside her in gardening overalls, laughing at something Rhi's dad was saying behind the bar.

"Lila!"

Rhi was waving, pushing through the crowd, hand in hand with her boyfriend Brody. She looked adorable in a playsuit printed all over with black and white music notes. Lila noticed a clef-shaped pendant on the leather necklace Brody wore around his neck.

"You two didn't have to dress up as anything," said Lila as Rhi hugged her and Brody and Josh shook hands. "Everyone knows you're going to be the most famous musicians ever to come out of Heartside Bay."

"Polly found this amazing fabric and promised to make me something to wear tonight, so I couldn't refuse," Rhi laughed back. "We're playing later. You should see the set Eve's rigged up for us behind the curtain. Then the summer will really begin. Brody and

I have so many gigs, I'm going to need another holiday by the time we get to September."

"November you mean," Brody corrected with a smile. "I got a call this morning booking us at the Stag's Head for Halloween. We're booked up right through until then."

Rhi clapped her hands and kissed Brody full on the lips.

Two more people who knew who they were and what they wanted to be. Lila couldn't help a feeling of doom. Eve was already planning parties most weekends with her business partner Caitlin. Ollie would come through the Heartbeat Café's doors any minute dressed as the professional footballer he'd wanted to be since he was about ten years old, and Polly would be next to him wearing one of her original designs from her upcycling label Turned Around With Love and looking incredible, and . . . here *she* was. Boring old Lila in a boring old dress, looking like nobody at all.

You have lots of waitressing over the summer doing Mr Gupta's weddings, she reminded herself. *Heartside Bay heaves with weddings every summer, that'll keep you busy.*

It was work, true enough. But it wasn't exciting, and it certainly wasn't what Lila wanted to be doing for the rest of her life. As Rhi and Brody headed for the stage, Lila sighed and adjusted the necklace she was wearing.

She felt Josh kiss her lightly on the temple. "You look absolutely beautiful tonight," he whispered in her ear. "I won't be able to keep my eyes off you."

Lila flushed with pleasure. "Really? You don't think I look boring? You don't think it matters that I'm not a scientist, or a dancer, or a judge or something like that?"

Josh kissed her on the lips. "I can't see you as any of those things, to be honest," he said. "And you'd hate being a judge. Those wigs are *so* unflattering."

That was true, Lila thought. She was pleased that Josh thought she looked good tonight, but she still felt out of sorts. *I should have come dressed as a bag lady,* she thought glumly. *That's about the only future I can picture right now.*

"Eve alert," said Josh suddenly. "I'd better get to work. Tonight's fee is paying for tomorrow's illustration course."

He kissed Lila one last lingering time and slid behind his caricature stand as Eve appeared with two mocktails in her hands, held high above the crowd. Her silver crown twinkled in the party lights strung overhead.

"I saw your glass was empty, Lila, and as any good host knows, that's the worst party crime in the world. Try this one, Rhi's dad designed it last week. We've called it Raspberry Résumé. I thought of the name," she added. "It has a lovely 'future career' ring to it, don't you think? What have you come as, then?"

Lila had been dreading that question. She opened her mouth, wondering what would come out.

"Are you a reality TV star?" Eve asked with a little laugh.

Lila flinched. That wasn't a compliment. She tried to make a joke of it, pouting her cherry-painted lips and striking a pose. "Maybe I could get my own show," she said, wiggling her hips from side to side. "Something like *The Blonde Game* would be good. I could give Lorna Lustre a run for her money."

Eve laughed with amusement, just as Lila had hoped she would. "Perfect," she said, in Lorna Lustre's trademark husky tones. "No talent required there at all. All you need to do is dye your hair and get a boob job."

"I loathe reality TV. It represents *everything* that's wrong with society."

Lila swung round, startled by the venom in Josh's tone. He was glaring at them both, frowning so hard that his eyebrows met in the middle.

"We're only joking," said Eve in surprise. "I'm sure Lila has more brains than to aim for a fake life in front of cameras twenty-four hours a day. Good luck with the drawings, I know you'll be marvellous."

Lila stared at Josh as Eve headed back to the bar. "Are you OK?"

He was muttering under his breath as he sharpened a pencil. "The whole reality TV bandwagon just gets up my nose."

Lila wound her arms around his neck. "Don't be angry, Josh. This is a party. I'd never be on a reality TV show, you know that." She grimaced. "My life wouldn't interest anyone."

She could feel the tension leaving him as she rubbed his shoulders with her hands. "It interests me," he said, looking down at her.

"You're biased because you're my boyfriend. No one else but you would want to hear about my life. Ooh, Lila wakes up and brushes her teeth. Lila goes to school! Wow, Lila hangs out at the Heartbeat, haunt of the rich and famous! Newsflash, Lila cuts her toenails at the kitchen table! I don't, by the way," she added hastily, not wanting Josh to think she was gross. "I cut them over the bin."

Josh's face twitched with a smile as he looked down at her. "Too much information."

Lila felt relieved that he looked happy again. "Forget I mentioned toenails," she said.

"You just mentioned them again."

"Doh," said Lila, whacking her forehead with the palm of her hand.

He laughed out loud at that. "Kiss me, toenail girl," he said.

Stop worrying about the future so much, Lila told herself as she kissed Josh. *You're in the here and now. You have a lovely boyfriend you've been dating for over a month, but it feels like for ever, in the best possible way. He treats you well and you love being with him. He's like your best friend and your boyfriend all rolled into one, and what could be better than that?*

"This is going to be a brilliant summer," she said firmly when Josh pulled back, his arms still looped around her back. "School's out, the sun is shining and we're going to have FUN."

Lila wished she could believe her own words. Even as Josh kissed her again, she felt uneasy. Everything had been going so well for her lately. It couldn't last. If living in a seaside town for the past few months had taught her anything, it was that tides flowed out as surely as they came in.

TWO

"Fast lane freak," Lila sang under her breath, her hands linked behind her head in the cool dry sand. "I ain't ashamed, I ain't ashamed, la la la." She propped herself up and flapped a hand under Josh's nose to get his attention. "Rhi and Brody were better than ever last night, weren't they? The crowd went so nuts for 'Fast Lane Freak', I thought the roof was going to come off."

Josh gently pushed Lila's hand out of the way. "They were brilliant, yes."

"And you were a total hit with your drawings. You must have drawn about fifty people. How many was it?"

"Lots," said Josh. He bent his head a little closer to his sketchbook.

"I loved Polly's dress," Lila continued. "She's doing so well with her market stall, have you heard? Turned Around With Love. It's such great idea, upcycling clothes. No one item of clothing is ever the same. She's going to do so well as a fashion designer, I know it. We should go and see her at her market stall one day and buy something."

"Hmm."

"I wish I knew what to do with my life. What do you think I should do, Josh?"

Josh looked at her over the tops of his glasses. "Lila," he said patiently, "you know how much I love to chat when I'm drawing. But is there any chance you could perhaps, I don't know – be quiet for a bit?"

"You're rubbish at chatting," Lila informed him, lying back on the sand again. They were in their favourite spot on the beach, a quiet stretch of sand that was located just where the beach started to curve to form the famous heart shape of Heartside Bay. It was far enough down the beach from the pier that it wasn't too crowded, but it provided the perfect vantage point from which to watch both halves of the bay. "I might as well chat to that seagull. Hello seagull, I like your hair."

The seagull looked at her suspiciously, and hopped a little further away.

"That's the one I was drawing," Josh sighed.

Lila giggled. "Whoops. He's still the same seagull, though. He's just further away. You should draw faster."

"You'll drive me mad one day," Josh said, leaning across and kissing her. His lips tasted salty, like the sea.

"Tell me honestly, Josh," said Lila. "What do you think I should do?"

"Stay very still."

"What?"

He had his sketchbook out again. "Do as you're told for once. As you've frightened my seagull away, I'm going to draw you instead. Close your eyes."

Lila obliged. The sea breeze felt cool against her face, and her eyelids glowed orange against the sun. "I wish you could make a career out of lying on beaches," she said after a few minutes. "I'd be really good at that."

"You're good at lots of things."

"Maybe I should work in the wedding industry. It's big business around here."

She opened one eye and squinted down the beach, where she could see one of Heartside Bay's customary wedding parties gathering at the edge of the water. A photographer was snapping another happy couple across the beach by the clock tower, while wedding guests in brightly coloured dresses, coats and hats hurried along the Marine Parade heading for one wedding or another, holding on tightly to their hats as the brisk sea breezes tried to tug them from their heads.

"You already work in the wedding industry, oh waitress of waitresses," Josh pointed out. "You can sit up now, I've finished."

As usual, Josh had captured her brilliantly with her hair spread out around her head on the sand. Her freckles and the little mole she had on one cheek were in exactly the right place. Lila wasn't sure she was nearly as pretty as Josh drew her, but she wasn't complaining.

"I prefer your seagull," she teased.

Josh put his sketchbook away and rested his arm on Lila's shoulders. "I don't. Kissing seagulls is no fun at all."

They kissed for a while. As Josh took out his sketchpad again and started a fresh picture of the white-sailed boats out in the bay, Lila leaned back against her rolled-up towel and watched the wedding party by the water's edge. The groom looked twice the bride's age, and seemed a little lost, standing to one side as his bride walked at the water's edge with her dress lifted daintily up to her knees. Lila wondered what had brought them together.

Maybe the bride was marrying him for his money. She would feed him a poisoned shrimp at the wedding breakfast and inherit his vast estates in Argentina the moment he died. It was perfect. He looked a bit poisoned already. Maybe she'd already done the evil deed. The image was so strong in her mind that she giggled out loud.

"What are you laughing at?" Josh asked, his eyes still trained on the boats out in the harbour.

"Nothing. Just something stupid I thought of."

"Stupid how?" When Lila told him, he grinned. "You have a wicked mind. Maybe they just fell in love like most people."

"That's boring." Lila studied the couple again. "I

bet he's blackmailing her into marrying him. Maybe he's a kind of Bond villain who's holding her extremely rich father hostage." She squinted up into the sky, where she could see a helicopter circling the bay. "Her father's in that helicopter right now, trussed up like a turkey. 'You must marry me now, Maria,'" Lila improvised in her best Russian accent, getting into the story she was telling, "'or my henchmen will throw your dear daddy to his death!'"

Josh laughed. "I have to draw that. Tell it again."

Lila embellished happily, filling in details as they occurred to her. Maria had met Mr Wrinkles on a cruise. Her father owned a huge diamond mine in Africa; Mr Wrinkles' lair lay deep beneath the polar ice caps. Josh's fingers flew across his sketchpad as Lila lost herself in the details.

"Maria is in love with Hans, of course, which makes everything worse," she informed Josh halfway through the story.

Josh paused. "Wait, who is Hans?"

"Maria's loved Hans since they were children." Lila pictured a meadow full of wild flowers, Maria and Hans running towards each other with their arms extended. "Hans has promised to save her on her wedding day. But he's late and it's all going wrong—"

To her delight, she noticed a tall man in sunglasses approaching the wedding party. He was a bit skinnier than she had imagined, and he had a very wet dog on a lead. Hardly the stuff of romantic legend, but he'd do.

"And here he is!" she said, sitting up straighter. "Hans himself!"

"Hans the hero doesn't have a very heroic dog," Josh pointed out.

"It's a killer dog," Lila said breezily. "Any minute now it's going to jump up at Mr Wrinkles and bite him to death." They both watched the soggy spaniel hurl itself into the sea, drenching half the wedding party. "It's just going swimming before its death mission," she added.

Josh was laughing so much he could hardly hold his pencil straight. Lila felt a warm glow deep in her belly. She loved making Josh laugh.

"That has to be your best-ever story," Josh said, wiping his eyes. "What do you think of this?"

Lila stared at the bold lines Josh had drawn. Mr Wrinkles in evil reflective sunglasses, Maria the bride wearing a glamorous wedding gown but with hate blazing in her eyes, Daddy in the helicopter. Hans the hero and his unheroic dog. She felt so envious of Josh's skill she could hardly breathe. *What must it be like to have a talent like his?* she wondered.

Josh pulled her into his arms. "You've gone quiet. Don't you like it?"

"It's brilliant," said Lila. She felt a little sad.

"I can't wait for my course to start," he said happily, making a few adjustments to the shading on Maria's bridal gown. "Mr Spiegelman's taking it up at the uni. I introduced you once. The old guy who owns the graphic-novel shop in the Old Town, do you remember? He's worked with all the greats. I'm going to learn so much with him."

Lila wondered if Josh would remember her when he was a famous illustrator and she was a nobody still waitressing at themed weddings, daydreaming her life away.

"It's only one day a week," Josh said, misreading her silence. "We'll have lots of fun together the rest of the holidays, just like you said at the party last night – I promise."

He reached for his sketchpad again, but Lila knocked it out of his hand. "No more drawing," she said, wrapping her arms around his neck and kissing him, deep and sweet.

She wished they could kiss for ever, and that the future would never come.

THREE

It was only ten o'clock on Monday morning, but Lila was already bored. She'd got used to the rhythms of school life, the regular trips to the Heartbeat and her days at the beach with Josh. Without school and without Josh, only the Heartbeat was left. Somehow she didn't think anyone would be hanging out there on a Monday morning.

She pictured Josh up at the uni, drawing up a storm and impressing everyone in the class. She wondered if any girls were taking the course with Josh, and instantly felt depressed. They would all be beautiful and talented and a lot more interesting than she was.

After taking the longest shower she could manage,

and spending half an hour longer on her hair and make-up than she normally did, Lila gave herself a talking-to in front of her bedroom mirror.

"You need to get a life," she told her reflection.

You think I don't know that? said her inner voice. It wasn't helpful.

"What are you up to today, love?" Lila's mother asked down in the kitchen.

Lila took a bite out of an apple from the fruit bowl as, finally, an idea came to her. "I thought I'd go and visit Polly at her market stall," she said. "I might look for something Tim or Alex would like, since they're coming up for your anniversary."

Her mother shook her head in wonder. "I can't believe I've been married to your dad for almost twenty-five years," she said. "Where did the time go?"

Lila thought about this as she walked into town. Where *did* time go? How could anyone lose track of twenty-five whole years?

The market was already busy when she arrived, the striped awnings shading shoppers from the bright July sunshine. Lila wandered between the shaded stalls, picking up plates and scarves and trinkets and putting them down again. She felt restless. Disconnected.

"Lila!"

Lila's mood improved at seeing Ollie waving at her beside Polly's stall.

"Nice choice, Ollie," she teased, pointing at the dress in Ollie's arms. "The colour will really bring out the blue in your eyes. You should try it on."

Ollie hung the dress – a pretty thing with a fitted white top with a strapless sweetheart neckline and full skirt in a deep dark blue – on a rail and wiped his hands down his trousers. "And scare off Polly's customers?" he said in a good-natured way. "I don't think so."

Lila could hardly see Polly for shoppers crowded around her rails. She waved to get Polly's attention. Polly flapped her hand in a distracted sort of way before a customer put their head around the small tented area she'd set up as a changing room and asked for the mirror.

"She's really busy," Ollie said proudly. "People can't get enough of Pol's designs."

Lila could see what Ollie meant. Already the blue dress had been snatched off the rail and was being "ooh"ed over by two girls she recognized from school. She felt the old stab of familiar envy. Lucky Polly, to be so good at this.

"Excuse me, what can you tell me about this piece?"

Ollie swung round. "Um," he said, gazing at the coral and gold necklace in the the customer's hand. "It goes around your neck, I think."

Lila had to giggle. As Ollie did his best to help the customer, she gazed at the next stall along. It was selling stationery: notebooks, pens, writing paper, cards and envelopes. She selected a card for her parents' anniversary first, then ran her hand over the brightly coloured woollen covers on the notebooks. Each one was different.

"Four ninety-nine," said the girl behind the stall, noting her interest. "I make the bindings myself from felt."

Lila picked up a book with a sea-green cover. The wavy lines of the felted cover reminded her of the tide turning in the bay, while the paper was thick and creamy coloured and faintly scored with lines. It felt heavy and solid in her hands. Perfect for a diary.

Any diary you wrote would be a riot, she thought wryly. *Got up, went to school, wondered about the future, went to bed, repeat for ever.*

She bought it anyway and tucked it into her bag beside the card.

It was no good trying to talk to Polly and Ollie now – the Turned Around With Love stall was busier than ever. Pulling out her phone and retreating to a quieter part of the market, Lila dialled Eve's number. Eve was always up for a bit of shopping and a gossip over a coffee.

"Hey," said Lila hopefully. "What are you up to?"

Eve's voice was faint through a loud thumping noise in the background. "Sorry babes, I can't hear you very well. Becca and I are auditioning bands for a big fundraiser Caitlin's organizing in London next week. I have indie rock coming out of my ears. Hello? Are you still there?"

Auditioning bands? That sounded like fun. Lila raised her voice. "Need any help?"

"Sorry darling, I can't hear a thing. I'll be at the

Heartbeat on Wednesday like we arranged, see you there at noon. I have some great new ideas to make your parents' secret wedding anniversary party go with a swing."

Eve rang off. *So much for shopping*, Lila thought a little grumpily.

Their parents' surprise party had been her brother Alex's idea. He'd rung Lila out of the blue a couple of weeks earlier to suggest it.

"We'll get all the aunties and uncles and friends they always write Christmas cards to but never see. Dad will go mental. He hates surprises."

Lila had giggled at the thought. "Dad takes himself too seriously. A party is just what he and Mum need. Do you think we should tell Tim? He's hopeless at keeping secrets."

"Leave our brother to me," Alex had said. "I'm better at threatening him than you are, he won't squeal. Know anyone who's good at planning parties?"

Lila had barely raised the idea with Eve at school before her friend was making lists and phoning people. Not for the first time, Lila was grateful to have Eve on her side. Everything was almost in place for the party, and they still had four days to go. Wednesday's meeting was all about finalizing the details.

It was midday, according to her phone. The day was dragging by like a snail.

Someone will be at the Heartbeat by now, she decided. *Rhi and Brody, most likely.*

Feeling energized again, Lila left the market and headed for the Old Town.

"Hi, Mr Wills," she said as she pushed open the café's wooden door. "Is Rhi around?"

Rhi's father looked up from restocking the bar with crisps. "She's in the usual place," he said, looking at the ceiling. "She and Brody have been singing up there since ten this morning."

Lila took the stairs two at a time, towards the rehearsal room in the attic. Outside, the sky was blue. She itched to get back outside and feel the warmth of the sun on her skin. She'd ask Rhi and Brody to join her at the beach.

It was hard to tell at first which of the two people wrapped up in each other's arms was Rhi and which was Brody. Lila froze, her palm still on the attic room's door handle. Keen not to disturb them and make an embarrassing scene, she tried to close the door again.

Rhi noticed first. "Lila!" she said, breaking off mid-kiss with an embarrassed giggle. "Sorry, you caught us, uh, rehearsing. How's it going?"

Brody twirled one of Rhi's curls between his fingers and smiled at Lila.

"OK," Lila said, feeling horribly embarrassed. "I just wondered if maybe . . . never mind."

"You want to hang out?" Brody asked. "We were about to run through a new song. Do you want to hear it?"

"Stay," said Rhi, holding out her hand to Lila.

But the last thing Lila wanted to be was a spare part today.

"Some other time," she said, closing the door. "Have fun."

She could hear them both laughing as she headed back down the stairs again.

She stood in the cobbled lane outside the Heartbeat Café's doors, and wondered what to do next. Everyone was busy. Everyone was getting on with their lives except her.

You wanted to go to the beach, she reminded herself.

Squaring her shoulders, she set off towards the silvery sand. So what if she was by herself? Loads of people walked on the beach by themselves every day. *Loads of friendless losers*, the voice whispered.

She sat on the beach in her and Josh's usual spot, her arms wrapped around her knees, and tried to think positive thoughts. It was hard. She found her mind drifting back to her old friends in London. Flynn and Iris and Leo. They'd be on their summer holidays now, same as she was.

Something stirred in her belly. She would text them, invite them to Heartside to visit over the summer. Pleased with the idea, she pulled out her phone.

Hey!!! Long time no speak.
Anyone fancy a trip to the beach?
Lil xx

Flynn responded first.

LILZ!! Too long, girl. Busy babes but will text SOOOOON
F xx

Leo was next.

Great to hear ur news xx

Lila frowned. She hadn't *given* Leo any news. It was clear he hadn't read her message properly.

Iris didn't respond at all. *She'll have lost her phone,* Lila decided as the time stretched away without a reply. *Iris is always losing her phone.*

Trying not to feel downhearted at the way her old friends were getting on with their lives without her, Lila tucked her phone into her bag and lay down on the sand to stare at the puffy white clouds drifting by overhead.

It was going to be a long afternoon.

FOUR

"Lila, I need you to *concentrate*," said Eve.

Lila jumped guiltily. She had been watching the café doors, waiting for Tim and Alex to arrive. They were late. "Sorry," she said.

"Anyone would think you're nervous about something," said Josh in amusement.

"You know perfectly well I'm nervous about you meeting my brothers," Lila said fretfully.

She loved Tim and Alex, but she knew how much they were going to tease her now they were going to meet her famous boyfriend at last. The last thing she needed was for those two idiots to scare away the best thing in her life.

"I'm sure we'll weather it," said Josh, and he kissed her.

Lila pushed him away. "Not here!" The thought of her brothers walking in and seeing her *kissing* . . . it was too embarrassing to think about.

"As I was *saying*," Eve said pointedly. She fluttered a list under Lila's nose. "In the absence of your brothers, we need to make a few decisions. So here we go. Beer or wine?"

"Both," said Lila.

Eve nodded and put a brisk tick on her list. "Canapés. We have savoury tomato, goat's cheese and pesto tartlets, chilli prawns, teriyaki chicken skewers, mushroom bruschetta, mini blinis and of course honey and mustard sausages. And loads of soft drinks, beer and wine. Has everyone replied?"

Lila looked at her own list. It was scruffier than Eve's, with lots of scribbles and crossings out. She wasn't very good at organizing things. *Something else I'd better not make a career of*, she thought gloomily. "Thirty-five definites, three maybes," she said out loud.

Eve looked at her. "Lila, you only invited twenty-seven people."

"Tim and Alex added some more at the weekend."

Eve made extra notes in the margins. *She was so cool*, Lila thought, lost in admiration for her stylish, unflappable friend. She'd make a much better host at the party than Lila would.

"Are you sure you won't come to the party, Eve?" she asked without thinking. "I could use your help on the night."

Eve shut her notebook. "I'm organizing this party as a favour to you," she said a little sharply. "Don't ask me for anything more than that."

Eve still hadn't forgiven Lila's father for arresting her dad, that much was clear. Lila and Eve had rebuilt their friendship after that particular scandal, but their fathers were still a subject best not discussed. Lila kicked herself for not thinking that particular question through.

"Sorry," she said quickly. "Of course. I was just saying . . . you'd be very welcome."

She jumped as the café door swung open again. *Tim and Alex*, she thought. *Finally*. But it was only Polly and Rhi, talking and laughing. Their appearance broke the awkward silence that had descended.

"Come on then," said Polly as Rhi fetched some drinks. "Let's see the memories."

Lila had emailed everyone on the party list asking them for memories of her parents. Polly had promised to help Lila put them all into a beautiful book, with Rhi's help as well. Lila had received some amazing things: old party invitations, photographs, concert tickets, postcards. Fumbling in her bag, she laid everything on the table. Her friends pounced.

"Oh my gosh, this so funny!" Polly giggled over a wedding photo. "Your dad is wearing a bow tie! And look at the frills on your mum's wedding dress!"

They all pored over the pictures and stories. Tales of someone pushing Lila's dad into a swimming pool, and her mother losing a shoe at university that had ended up on top of a bus shelter. Nearly all of the pictures showed Lila's mother in hilarious eighties outfits and hair.

"Look at your mother's *perm*!" Eve said in horror, peering at the pictures.

"Mum swears it was fashionable in her time," Lila grinned. "Josh is going to do some caricatures of Mum and Dad to include in the book as well. What do you think?"

"It's going to be gorgeous and your parents will *love* it," Polly promised. "Leave it to me and Rhi."

Lila made a triumphant tick on her scruffy to-do list. Here at least she'd managed to do something right.

They fetched more drinks. It was lovely sitting here with all her friends, Lila thought, talking and laughing and squabbling as only friends could. Eve, witty and dry and full of gossip. Josh full of enthusiasm for his illustration course, showing the others some of the work he'd been doing in his sketchbook. *When Tim and Alex come, it'll be just as Josh says*, she assured herself. *We'll be fine.*

"So," said Eve, leaning back in her chair, "who has summer plans? Rhi?"

"Only what you already know. Singing with Brody," said Rhi, smiling. "Mainly around Heartside Bay, but we have a few gigs further down the coast in August."

"Lila?"

"Just hanging out, really," Lila said, feeling a little lame. "Going with the flow."

"I have a plan," said Polly, stirring her frappé.

"Making your first million in the market?" said Eve.

Polly's eyes gleamed. "Better than that. Ollie and I are going to America!"

Everyone gasped. Lila felt a jolt of envy. America? She'd always wanted to go there.

"Wow!" Rhi cried. "You sneaky thing, you never said!"

"I didn't know if I'd have enough money for the plane tickets," said Polly. "But the stall's been going so well, I've got enough for both me and Ollie to fly out to California. We're going to visit my dad on his farm out there."

"Oh my gosh, that's amazing!" Rhi gushed.

"That's brilliant, Polly," said Josh admiringly.

"You *have* to go to Newport Beach, darling," said Eve, leaning forward. "So glamorous. I'll give you a list of restaurants."

Lila felt a searing stab of envy. Polly was going to America, while all she had to look forward to was boring old Heartside Bay. She sat silently in her chair, her good mood evaporating, as the others discussed all the things Polly and Ollie would be able to do on their holiday. She knew she should be glad for her friends, but it wasn't fair. Why didn't exciting things ever happen to her?

She gave herself a talking-to in the bathroom.

"Polly deserves this," she told the mirror. "She's been working really hard, and she hasn't seen her dad for months." Her tousle-haired, blue-eyed reflection gazed sullenly back at her. *So what?* it seemed to say. *It's still not fair.*

Polly came into the bathroom, making Lila jump. *Don't rain on Polly's parade*, she ordered herself. *She deserves more than that from you.*

"So," she made herself say. "Are you excited about going to the States?"

Polly filled her lips with her favourite bright-red lipstick. "Nervous, mainly," she admitted, popping the lid back on.

Lila was surprised. "What about?"

"Flying. Introducing Ollie to Dad." Polly grimaced a little. "That is going to be seriously weird. What if they don't get on?"

"I know what you mean," Lila found herself saying. "Josh is meeting Tim and Alex for the first time today. I'm a little freaked out about it."

"They were all getting on fine when I left them," Polly said casually, putting her lipstick back in her bag.

Tim and Alex were *here*?

Lila hurtled back into the bar. Her brothers both had their arms tightly locked around Josh's neck. It looked like they were strangling him.

"Dating our little sister, huh?" said Tim into Josh's ear.

"We hope you're playing nice," said Alex.

"Get off him, you idiots," said Lila diving between them and pulling them off her boyfriend with some difficulty.

"It's OK, Lila," said Josh. "I don't need rescuing."

Alex dropped into a chair and slung his arm around Josh's shoulders. "No offence, mate," he said affably, "but you're stronger than you look. Sorry we're late. Big uni party last night. It was tough getting out of bed. How are the party plans?"

"Party," said Tim happily. He'd put his arm around Eve, who didn't look very pleased about it.

Lila loved Tim and Alex, but they could be impossible. "Get your hands off Eve, Tim, or you're likely to lose that arm," she said out loud. "Have you arranged things for Mum and Dad for Friday during the day?"

"Lila has everything else under control," Josh put in.

"Somehow I find that hard to believe," said Alex.

"Hey!" Lila objected, punching her older brother lightly on the arm. "I have actually, ask the others."

Eve, Polly and Rhi nodded. *See?* Lila wanted to say.

"OK, so we're going to rock up just before lunch and take the olds for fish and chips along the coast," Tim said. "We thought it would be better to keep them out of Heartside Bay for the afternoon. If they saw all their cousins and friends streaming through town, they might ask questions. When do you want us back again?"

Lila consulted her list. "The party starts at—"

"Seven," said Josh.

"We're allowing for thirty-eight guests but might only have thirty-five," Lila continued. "We're having nibbles. Tartlets, blinis, mushroom bruschetta, sausages, p—"

"Prawns, some chicken things," said Josh promptly.

"Does your boyfriend finish all your sentences?" Alex asked, laughing.

"Course he does," said Tim, coming back from the

bar with an armful of crisps. "He and our baby sister are like an old married couple already."

Lila's friends giggled as Tim and Alex made kissy-kissy noises. Josh laughed, taking it in good humour, but Lila felt annoyed. She was only fifteen. How was she part of a boring old married couple already?

FIVE

"It's so nice having everyone for dinner like this," said Lila's mother. She sighed. "Such a shame that you boys have to go back to university on Friday afternoon. It would have been nice to celebrate together in the evening."

"Never mind, Mum," said Alex. He helped himself to more macaroni cheese. "At least Tim and I are taking you and Dad out for lunch on Friday before we have to head back."

Liar, Lila thought. Her brothers both looked so innocent, so sorry that they had to get back to uni. That they couldn't change their plans, even for their own parents' twenty-fifth wedding anniversary. Tim was usually a pretty hopeless liar, but he was doing well tonight. It couldn't last. She really hoped no one cracked. They'd put too much work into keeping the party a secret for it to be ruined now.

"Leave some of that for our guest," said Lila's dad a little sharply as Alex started to scrape around the edges of the macaroni dish.

"Josh is all right," said Alex, shamelessly taking the last crusty bits of pasta for himself. "Aren't you, Joshy boy?"

"He's too fat anyway," said Tim. He pinched at Josh's long, slender arm jokingly. "Needs to lose a good five stone, I'd say. Water and dry bread for you, boy."

"That's all you'll be getting when you marry our sister, Josh," Alex said. "Lila's never spent much time in the kitchen."

"Apart from when she's stealing biscuits," said Tim.

"And hearts," Josh said. He kissed Lila's hand, smiling at her.

Tim rolled his eyes and stuck his fingers down his throat. Lila's mum and dad smiled knowingly at each other. Lila resisted the urge to snatch her hand away. This was all too embarrassing.

"Ah, Joshy," said Alex, shaking his head. "Set the date, why don't you? Tim can be your bridesmaid."

Josh looked thoughtful. "I can't see you in peach satin, Tim. Mauve, maybe."

Alex and Tim both roared at that one.

Josh looked like he was loving every minute. It was strange seeing him in the thick of her family like this. Her boyfriend was the least sociable person at Heartside High, and generally went out of his way to avoid a conversation. He was different here.

"Lil," said Tim absently, drawing pictures on his plate in what was left of his ketchup. "Is Auntie K—"

Lila kicked him hard. Tim's eyes widened as he realized what he'd almost said. *Is Auntie Kay coming to the party?*

"Is antique what?" asked their mother.

Josh managed to turn a snort of very obvious laughter into a cough. Lila wanted to kick him too.

"Yes, Tim," Alex said, smiling wickedly at his younger brother. "What were you going to say about antiques?"

"Um," said Tim, looking nervous. "They are . . . old. Very old."

"Nearly as old as me," Lila's dad remarked. He wiped his mouth with his napkin.

"What were you thinking?" Lila hissed at her younger brother as her father pushed back his chair and helped Josh clear the plates.

"I was thinking about macaroni, mainly," Tim confessed with a grimace. "Sorry, Lil. Won't happen again."

"It'd better not," Alex whispered, kicking his little brother under the table.

"What are you three whispering about?" Their mother was back, setting a bowl of trifle on the table.

"Nothing," said Lila quickly. She needed to divert this conversation. "That trifle looks fantastic, Mum. Can I have some?"

"Oh no you don't," said Alex, lifting the bowl out of Lila's reach. "Not if you want to fit into your wedding dress, little sister."

Lila gave him a glare and stole back the bowl of trifle, scooping an enormous portion on to her plate and sticking out her tongue at Alex. More wedding jokes. It was unnerving, the way her brothers kept harping on about her and Josh getting married. Was that going to be the sum total of her future? Being someone's wife?

I want to be more than that, she thought. *I don't want to be one of those girls that gets married, has kids and then wakes up in twenty years' time wondering what happened.*

If only it was as easy to know what she *did* want.

"That one's getting a little stale, Alex," she muttered. "Shut up will you?"

Alex called Josh back to the table. "Seeing how you're going to marry our sister," he began, grinning, "you'd better tell us your prospects, Josh. Will you keep her in the style to which she is accustomed? She has expensive habits."

"They can't be any more expensive than mine," said Josh, grinning back. "Have you seen the price of sketchpads lately?"

"Does your family live in Heartside Bay?" Alex asked through a mouthful of trifle. "Are they artists too, is that where you get this weird urge to draw stuff?"

"Manners, Alexander," said Lila's dad a little pointedly. "Josh doesn't want to see that trifle disappearing down your throat."

"I live with my grandfather in the Old Town," said Josh.

"Why, where are your mum and dad?" Tim asked.

Lila wanted a hole to open in the floor and swallow her up. Josh never talked about his parents. He'd never even told *her* about them. Couldn't her brother see how uncomfortable Josh was looking?

"Thanks for dinner, Mum," she said, standing up abruptly, keen to get out of the room and away from all the questions. "Josh, let's go upstairs."

"Don't do anything we wouldn't do!" Alex shouted after them as she dragged Josh up the stairs and shut the bedroom door to the sound of raucous laughter.

"Sorry about that." Lila could feel her face turning scarlet. "Alex and Tim are. Alex and Tim, basically."

Josh sat at her desk with his hands behind his head. "Don't worry about it. Are you OK?"

"Of course I'm OK, why wouldn't I be OK?" Lila demanded.

He shrugged. "I don't know. You tell me."

She hated that he could read her so well. *You two are like an old married couple already. . .*

She sat on the bed. Then she stood up again and

paced around the room, picking things up and putting them down again. She was feeling really weird.

"Talk to me, Lila," said Josh.

"I don't want to talk," she muttered. She rubbed her temples with her fingers. "Sorry Josh, I'm suddenly . . . not feeling very sociable. I'm nervous about the party, I think. About it all going wrong. Maybe I'm just tired. I should get some sleep."

He stood up at once and kissed her on the cheek. "It'll be OK. Get some rest and try not to worry. I'll head home then and we can hang out tomorrow."

Why did he have to be so understanding? It made Lila feel guilty in some strange way for these – doubts she was having.

Was that what they were? Doubts about her and Josh?

"That would be nice," she said.

She tried to relax as he took her in his arms and kissed her goodbye. She couldn't.

SIX

Lila had almost bitten her fingernails to the quick as she answered the doorbell for the fifth time in as many minutes. If anyone had told her how hard organizing a secret party would be, she'd never have started. Even though it was completely different from the types of parties she used to throw in London, the idea of mixing her parents and parties still made her feel a bit sick. She just hoped they would like it.

"Hello Lila, dear." Auntie Kay kissed her. She smelled of coffee and perfume. "Goodness, isn't the house looking nice? When are the victims coming home?"

"Fifteen minutes," said Lila anxiously. "Go through to the living room, Auntie Kay. Everyone's in there. But don't draw the curtains, OK? I don't want Mum and Dad to see you all when Tim and Alex bring them back."

"You have my word," said Auntie Kay, tapping her heavily powdered nose. "Do you know," she added suddenly, "your uncle threw a surprise party for my fortieth birthday? I was furious."

Lila felt a little sick. "You were?"

"I was wearing my oldest gardening dungarees while all the guests were dressed up to the nines. I felt like such a fool." Auntie Kay sighed and shook her head. "Men so often don't think about these things."

Lila tried to remember what her mother had been wearing when Tim and Alex had whisked her parents away. Luckily her mother wasn't too bothered by clothes, not like Auntie Kay and her beautiful dresses and shoes. She grimaced as she thought about poor Uncle Toby and how much trouble he must have been in.

Along with the nerves about the party, Lila was wrestling with a sense of guilt. She'd told so many lies that week, she could hardly look herself in the eye in the bathroom mirror any more. The sad look on her mother's face as she'd scooped up her bag and keys shortly before lunch had been almost more than Lila could stand.

"Are you sure you can't join us, love? It won't be the same with just Tim and Alex."

"Cheers, Mum," said Alex.

"That makes us feel really wanted," Tim added.

Lila's mother had flapped her hands at the pair of them. "I don't mean . . . oh, you two are impossible."

Lila crossed her fingers behind her back. "Sorry Mum, I promised to help Polly with her market stall today," she lied.

Her father helped her mum put on her jacket. "Come on, Jane," he'd said. "I can smell those fish and chips already."

You'll feel better when the party starts, Lila told herself.

The doorbell went again.

"Sorry I'm late," said Polly, coming through the door. "Is there loads still to do?"

"Rhi is in the kitchen organizing the canapés," Lila said. "The guests have drunk loads already. What if we run out of wine before Mum and Dad get back?"

Polly patted her on the shoulder. "Eve knows what

she's doing," she reassured Lila. "Nice dress, by the way."

Lila grinned and smoothed down the short pink floral dress with its old Victorian buttons. "I got it from this great little market stall I know," she joked. "Turned Around With Love. Have you heard of it?"

Polly laughed. "It looks gorgeous on you. Where's Josh?"

"Schmoozing with the olds in the living room."

Lila's aunts and uncles couldn't get enough of Josh, judging from the laughter coming from the living room. Lila wasn't sure how she felt about that.

Polly vanished into the kitchen to help Rhi load up the trays with canapés. Lila hovered by the front door, peering through the glass panels for the first sign of her parents' return. The moment she glimpsed her father's jacket through the hedge at the front of the house, Lila shot into the living room and waved her arms.

"They're here!" she hissed. "Everyone quiet!"

The room fell as quiet as a mouse. Through the living-room door, Lila glimpsed Polly and Rhi frozen to the spot in the kitchen, holding their trays of canapés. The keys opened in the door. Lila heard her mother say, "Who put this banner up in the hall? Where did all these balloons come from?"

The room erupted as Lila's parents came through the living-room door.

"SURPRISE!" everyone shouted, lifting their glasses up in the air.

"Goodness," said Lila's father, sitting down very suddenly on the sofa as his brother, two nephews, half a dozen cousins and several close friends from the police station swarmed around him for handshakes and kisses. "Not much of a copper am I? I didn't suspect a thing!"

"This is all your daughter's fault!" Auntie Kay shouted, in the thick of the laughing throng surrounding Lila's mother. "We should congratulate her on a job well done!"

Lila blushed as the room turned to face her and applaud.

Her mother had tears in her eyes as she gathered Lila into a hug. "Goodness, you sly old thing," she said. "Working on Polly's market stall indeed!"

Josh went around the room filling everyone's glasses with champagne as Polly and Rhi came in bearing silver trays. Lila's mother kept bursting into tears with every new face she spotted in the room.

"David! Goodness me, this can't be Lucy, can it? You were two last time we saw you. Sophie! *Pippa?*"

"A toast," shouted Alex over the hubbub. "To our parents, Greg and Jane. The best parents in the world. Twenty-five years together and they best they could produce was us three." He shook his head in sorrow. "They did their best, I suppose."

The room roared at that. Alex raised his glass.

"May your waistlines never expand, your hairlines never recede and your bank balance never let you down. Happy anniversary!"

"Happy anniversary!" the room echoed.

Lila's mother was crying again. Lila pushed through the throng, holding the memory book close to her chest. Polly had wrapped it so beautifully in purple tissue paper, it seemed a shame to unwrap it. But her mother unwrapped it on the spot, and fresh tears began to fall almost immediately.

"Oh!" she gasped, leafing through the book with its photographs, notes and postcards, each page decorated with Josh's caricatures. "Lila darling . . . this is incredible. Where did you get all of this? How did you make such a lovely thing? Greg, you have to see this!"

"You've done very well, love," said Lila's father, gathering her into his arms for a kiss. "I'm proud of you."

That makes a change, thought Lila. *We moved to Heartside Bay six months ago for precisely the opposite reason.*

"Congratulations, Chief Murray," said Josh, shaking her father's hand.

"Call me Greg, Josh, for heaven's sake," her father replied with a smile. "First-name terms is the least I can do for the boy who's made my daughter so happy."

Lila glanced around the living room, at all the smiling faces and the lively chatter. It was all so familiar, so safe. So predictable. So *nice*. Including Josh. Lila found it hard to remember what London had been like.

Her fingers went to the small tattoo on her wrist, tracing the flowing blue lines. The tattooist had disguised her old boyfriend's initials as best he could when he remade the tattoo, but Lila could still make them out in the swirling pattern. Her belly stirred as she remembered the fun she and Santiago'd had. He'd been wild and impetuous, spontaneous and fun, and her parents had hated him. She'd enjoyed that her parents had hated him. He had been the exact opposite of Josh in every way.

She needed some air. Slipping out of the living room, she went into the kitchen and pushed open the doors to the garden. The breeze was cool on her face.

Is this what my life will be like in twenty-five years' time? she wondered, gnawing at her lip. *A little house, a handful of friends? A book of postcards to remember the past?*

Her parents were happy, but a life like theirs wasn't enough for her. She didn't want to turn out the same way. She didn't want life to be *nice*. She wanted a life that was full of excitement.

Josh's smiling face floated into her head. His bright green eyes, his gentle kisses.

You're lucky to have a boyfriend like Josh, she reminded herself. *He's reliable, honest, trustworthy . . . but was that enough?*

SEVEN

Lila stirred restlessly. The sand was sticking to her legs today, and blowing into her eyes.

"Stay still, can't you?" Josh's pencil was a blur against his sketchpad. "Screwed up eyes is not a look you want immortalized – trust me."

Lila wondered a little irritably how many drawings Josh had of her. Hundreds, probably. More than enough. She stood up, shaking the sand out of her hair. "I'm not in the mood for this today," she said abruptly.

Josh folded up his sketchbook and studied her. "What's going on? You've been like a cat with tar on its paws all day."

Wasn't it obvious? They were on the beach on a

Saturday afternoon, *again*. Josh was drawing her, *again*. Lila was so bored and restless, she felt like screaming.

"I'm going for a walk," she said.

"Want some company?"

Josh's company was the last thing she wanted right now. She shook her head. "Find a seagull to draw." She spread her arms. "There are plenty to choose from."

She could hear how peevish she sounded, but she didn't care. Pulling her cardigan on, she stomped off down the beach towards the edge of the water. The endless crashing of the surf didn't help her mood. Was *everything* around here on repeat?

Maybe if I wish it hard enough, she thought as she stared out at the glittering sea, *a boat might appear and whisk me away.*

She could picture it clearly. It would be a sleek red boat with a bright rainbow sail and a handsome stranger with a devilish smile at the tiller. He would look a bit like Santiago.

"Let's go," he would say.

"Where to?" she would reply, taking his hand as he helped her into the boat.

His smile would grow wider. "Who knows? Somewhere else."

Like that's ever going to happen, Lila thought sourly. Josh was never happier than when he was sitting on the beach with her and his sketchpad. He would do it every day if he could. He'd never turn up in a boat. He'd never *surprise* her.

She paced along the beach, her eyes flitting restlessly over all the families huddled around their picnic blankets, their sandcastles, their deckchairs. None of them looked like they were having the time of their lives. Half of the kids had snot dripping from their noses. Most of the mothers looked as fed up as she felt. They would all have been as young as her once. She wondered if they had ever stood at the edge of the water and dreamed of mysterious strangers whisking them away to more interesting lives.

I don't want to dream about life, she thought in desperation. *I want to make life happen.*

She walked silently back to Josh. He smiled at her, holding out his latest sketch.

"What do you think?"

Another seagull. Lila wanted to cry with frustration.

"What do you want me to say, Josh?" she said sarcastically. "Nice feathers?"

He slid the sketchpad into his bag and stood up. "What's the matter with you today?"

"Nothing," Lila muttered. "I want to go home. I'm waitressing at a wedding with Polly tonight at Heartwell Manor. I need a shower. Can we go?"

Josh took her hand, but she pulled away. Looking hurt, he put his hands in his pockets instead. They walked home in silence.

Concentrating hard, Lila stacked the little white meringues into pyramids on the silver trays. They looked very pretty, like miniature snowy mountains. Lila could almost picture tiny skiers hurtling down their shiny white sides, yelling at each other in high-pitched voices as they sped towards the silver trays.

Not silver trays, frozen lakes, covered in fresh snow, Lila thought, caught up in the image in her mind. She imagined the spray of snow the skiers would make when they reached the bottom and turned quickly to stop. It was almost a shock to feel the hard silver surface of the tray with her fingers.

The marquee was the most beautiful Lila had ever seen. She had waitressed at several weddings in Heartside Bay's most exclusive venue, but this one topped all the others. Everything was white: the flowers, the tablecloths, the candles, the napkins. The meringues. The only flash of colour was the deep green leaves of the white peonies on the tables. Outside in the Heartwell Manor gardens, rows of white chairs had been set up beside a white pergola covered in a climbing white rose, ready for the ceremony. Standing to one side of the pergola was a large cage full of white doves, ready to be released as the couple exchanged their vows.

"No prizes for guessing what colour the bride and groom will be wearing," Polly joked. Her own white dress suited her, nipped in at the waist in the vintage style she loved, with a white rose tucked behind one ear.

"As long as the groom doesn't confuse us with his bride!" Lila said. She was dressed the same as Polly, but she had pinned her white rose to her bodice.

"Edward only has eyes for Stephanie," said Polly dreamily. "I know them," she explained at Lila's startled expression. "Well, I know Edward anyway. He works with Mum at the estate agency."

The first guests started arriving, settling themselves down in the chairs and chattering among themselves. To Lila's astonishment, they were all wearing white as well. The effect was like something out of *Alice in Wonderland*. She watched them as the seats filled up, a sea of white in the green garden.

Thoughts of Josh had been plaguing her all afternoon. She needed Polly's advice.

"I need to talk to you Polly," she whispered as more and more white-clad guests settled down in the garden chairs, studying the white orders of service with their white ribbons.

"I need to talk to you too," Polly said. "We have to plan some amazing double dates for when Ollie and I get back from America."

"It's about me and Josh," Lila blurted.

"What about you and Josh?"

Lila had no idea where to start. "You know my tattoo?" she said at last.

Polly frowned. "What?"

Maybe the tattoo wasn't the best way to explain

the jumbled way she was feeling. But she had to start somewhere. Lila opened her mouth to try again.

"Listen," said Polly, "do you and Josh want to join me and Ollie in London when we get back? I thought we could have a picnic in one of the parks, maybe check out a market or two. What do you think?"

"That sounds lovely," said Lila helplessly. "But—"

There was a sudden commotion up at the manor behind the marquee. Turning round, Lila couldn't quite believe what she was seeing.

The bride was running at full tilt through the gardens, her veil flowing behind her like white smoke. Holding up her vast meringue-like skirts in both hands, she hurdled a low box hedge, ducked underneath some trailing vines and skidded into the white rose pergola. Her face, now Lila could see it more clearly, was as white as her dress.

"I'm sorry," she gasped at the shocked guests, half of whom had jumped out of their seats for a better view of the action. "So sorry. . ."

She swerved away from the pergola and raced onwards. As she passed the white doves, her stiff petticoats caught the cage and sent it toppling to the ground with a crash. The wired door flew open on impact. In a perfect moment of pure drama, doves exploded into the blue sky in a snowstorm of feathers.

This couldn't be happening.

Lila clutched Polly's arm in shock as half the wedding guests gave chase, led by the bridegroom, ploughing through the flowerbeds after the disappearing bride. "Stephanie!" she could hear someone calling in despairing tones. The groom, she guessed. Polly had said his name was Edward. "Steph, it's going to be OK . . . Steph, come back, talk to me. . ."

In a matter of moments, the perfect wedding scene had been smashed to pieces. Chairs were on their sides, wedding service sheets lay crumpled underfoot. Roses had been knocked from the pergola in the rush, scattering petals over the smooth green grass. Half the doves were still flapping overhead, the rest having come to roost on the pergola and in the hedges. The few guests who remained looked at each other with dazed expressions, holding on to their white fascinators and still clutching their orders of service.

Mr Gupta strode into the marquee.

"Time to clear up," he said grimly, clapping his hands. "Quickly now. I will of course pay for your time."

"But they might come back," said Polly weakly.

Taking a large white handkerchief from the top pocket of his white dinner jacket, Mr Gupta mopped his forehead. "They aren't coming back. The wedding is cancelled."

Lila stared at the trays of meringues that she'd so painstakingly arranged only moments ago. "What about the food?" she said.

"Get rid of everything," said Mr Gupta with a helpless shrug. "These things happen, girls. . ."

Tears flooded down Polly's cheeks as she looked around at the beautiful empty marquee and the ruined garden. "This is horrible," she sobbed. "Poor Edward. He's such a nice guy, Mum says. How could Stephanie run out on him on their *wedding* day? It must be the most humiliating thing in the world. Not only are you being dumped, you're being dumped in front of everyone you know and care about. It's awful."

Lila could still see the bride's white, stricken face in her mind. She had looked terrified. Something major must have propelled her down the garden like that. The realization that *this was the rest of her life*.

"If the bride realized he wasn't right for her, then it was better for everyone that she stopped the wedding," she said out loud. "Don't you think?"

Polly wiped her eyes with a napkin from the nearest table. "Some people don't know what they have until it's gone," she said.

Lila put away the clean plates and glasses. She swept the floor, helped box up the unburnt candles, folded the tablecloths, stacked the chairs. And as she worked, the same uncomfortable question spun through her head.

Am I one of those people?

EIGHT

"See you later, sis," Tim said, hugging Lila tightly.

"Be good," added Alex.

"This is Lil we're talking about," Tim reminded his older brother.

"Fine," said Alex without missing a beat. "Be bad but don't get caught." His hug lifted Lila off the station platform so that her feet dangled in the air. "You did well organizing that party," he said as he set her down again, "but don't make a habit of it. Mum and Dad will start expecting great things from the black sheep of the family."

"Keep their expectations low," said Tim cheerfully. "That way, no one gets disappointed. Works for me."

The joke was a little too close to the bone for

Lila's liking. "I'll do my best," she said, and tried to smile.

Alex clapped his hands to his head. "Not your *best*, you fool. Didn't you hear a word I said?" He extended a hand in Josh's direction. "Take care, man. I like you, sad to say."

As Josh joked with her brothers, Lila glanced wistfully around the platform, envying all the other travellers. Their lives were bound to be more interesting than her own.

The young couple by the departures board were leaving for the South of France, she decided. Their matching suitcases were a wedding present from an eccentric uncle who had left them an apartment in Monte Carlo after he died of a rare tropical disease. The two ladies were explorers, off to research a lost tribe in the Amazon. The old guy reading the paper on the bench didn't even seem interested in boarding the train. Perhaps he was a spy, Lila thought idly, waiting for a master criminal to reveal himself with a limp, or a spotted umbrella.

Josh put his arm around Lila as Tim and Alex boarded the train, and waved as they pulled away. As her brothers vanished around a curve in the track, Lila felt flatter than ever.

"So," said Josh, looking down at her. "What do you want to do?"

Lila laced her fingers through his. "Something *different*," she said fiercely. "I want to see different people, have conversations I've never had before. . ." An idea struck her. "How about spending the rest of the day at your house? You've met my entire family now, and I haven't met any of yours."

Josh looked worried. "Wouldn't you prefer to go to a café or something?"

"No," said Lila firmly. The more she thought about her suggestion, the more she liked it. "Let's go and hang out with your grandfather."

"He's busy," said Josh.

Lila frowned. "What's he doing?"

"He's always out on Sundays."

Lila looked disbelievingly at him. "He must be there sometimes."

Josh fiddled with his ear, a nervous habit Lila had noticed recently. "He goes fishing on Sundays with his buddies."

"Shall we go and say hi at the beach?" asked Lila. She hadn't even cared about hanging out with his grandfather until Josh had seemed so reluctant to let her meet him. Was he embarrassed by her?

She took Josh's hand and tried to lead him out of the station. Josh wouldn't budge.

This was getting weird now. Lila let go, put her hands on her hips and stared at him.

"What's going on, Josh?" she demanded. "Why don't you want me to meet your grandfather?" A horrible thought struck her. "Are you ashamed of me or something?"

Josh looked horrified. "No! Not at all! It's just . . . my home life is complicated at the moment, I can't explain. . ." He stopped and stared distractedly at the railway tracks. "I'll take you to meet my grandfather this week, I promise," he said, still staring at the curving steel rails. "Just . . . don't ask me today."

Lila's imagination had gone into overdrive. "Is everything all right at home?" She was almost afraid of what he might tell her.

Josh rubbed his eyes. "Everything's fine. Shall we go to the beach?"

Lila brushed his suggestion away. "I don't want to go to the beach. I want to know what's bugging you."

Josh's mouth had a stubborn set to it. "I told you, everything's fine. You'll meet Grandpa next week, I'll fix it up tonight. Let's make a decision about today before the weather changes. Those clouds look ominous."

He was trying to change the subject. Lila's curiosity deepened. What was he hiding? Why didn't he ever talk about his family? "Josh—" she started.

"Not today," he repeated. He leaned down and kissed her, and Lila almost forgot what they'd been talking about.

"How about we hang out here?" he suggested after a few minutes, squinting around at the station. "I could use a change of scenery for my sketches."

Lila knew when she was beaten. *We'll talk about this again*, she vowed to herself. *And soon.* She looked around at the coming and going of the passengers, their luggage and their pets and their strangely shaped packages. It could be fun, she supposed. It was somewhere different, anyway. And it looked like the best she was going to get today.

Josh settled himself down at an empty bench and took out his sketchpad. "Maybe you could help me," he said.

Lila pulled herself out of her brooding thoughts. "How?"

"Pick someone for me to draw."

More people were already starting to gather, people who had arrived early for the next train or late for the last one. It was easy to tell the difference. The late ones muttered and pulled out their phones and the early ones ambled off towards the coffee kiosk at the far end of the platform like they had all the time in the world.

"Her," Lila suggested, pointing at a middle-aged woman with a suitcase. She had a distracted air about her, and was wearing a large red hat.

"Perfect. Now tell me her story."

"I don't know her," Lila pointed out, feeling a little startled as she sat beside Josh on the bench.

Josh laughed. "Make something up! You're good at that. Help me pin a character down as well as a face."

Lila studied the woman more closely. The suitcase was battered, but the hat was new. What did that tell her?

"Dorothy Watkins is a lonely spinster leaving Heartside Bay in search of adventure," she said, visualizing the lady's imaginary life. "She's been living alone with her mother and a three-legged cat called Andrew and now her mother has died and Andrew has run away—"

Josh quirked his eyebrows. "I've never met a cat called Andrew. Never met a cat with three legs either."

"Do you want to hear how this story ends?" Lila demanded. "Dorothy has an old atlas in that suitcase. It's her prize possession, and it's full of Post-it Notes detailing all the places she wants to see around the world. It's a bit cat-eared—"

"*Cat*-eared?"

"Andrew chewed it," Lila explained. "He lost his leg when Dorothy slammed the atlas on him by mistake one day. He's hated the atlas ever since, obviously."

Josh's shoulders were shaking with laughter as he drew Dorothy Watkins and Andrew the three-legged cat and the world atlas. "What happens next?"

Lila could feel the end of the story rushing towards her like a light at the end of a dark tunnel. "Dorothy is so excited by her plans that she goes out and buys a wonderful red hat to celebrate her new adventurous self. But . . . I'm sorry to tell you that when the time comes to leave, she picks up the wrong suitcase."

"No!" Josh said.

"There are two identical suitcases in the hallway." Lila felt genuinely sad for Dorothy Watkins. "The atlas, wrapped carefully in tissue paper, is in one of them."

Josh's fingers were flying. "What's in the other one?"

It felt so obvious to Lila, she wondered why Josh had to ask. "Andrew didn't run away at all," she said. "He curled up in a nice quiet suitcase. . ."

"No!" Josh exclaimed again.

"Yes. Dorothy Watkins is taking Andrew on her adventure by mistake. Without her atlas, Dorothy Watkins loses her courage. She ends her days in another seaside town a bit like Heartside Bay, wistfully watching the boats depart for South America and Africa and New Zealand without her as Andrew sleeps on the window sill, using her red hat as a cushion."

Lila realized she was staring at the fictitious Dorothy Watkins' suitcase, convinced that she could hear a faint miaowing from inside. Imagination was a crazy thing.

"Lila, that's brilliant," Josh said.

She tore her eyes from the suitcase. "It's nothing," she said. "Just a silly story to help you visualize your character."

Josh flipped through his sketchbook and tore out a blank sheet of paper. "Will you do me a favour? Will you write that story down for me? I'll use it to work up the details on my sketches."

Lila doubtfully took the paper. "Sure," she said. "If you want."

NINE

Lila stared at the ceiling as the morning light washed through the curtains and across her bedroom. Monday again. Josh would go to his illustration class and she would do . . . what, exactly?

Last Monday had dragged by. Lila couldn't see today being any better. Polly and Ollie would be working at the market, Eve and Becca would be doing stuff together, Rhi and Brody would be singing. . . Everyone had their routines, and none of them included her.

It's good for you to be away from Josh sometimes, she reminded herself, thinking of all the married jibes her brothers had been throwing at her that weekend. She had to have her own interests, her own life. When she thought of spending day after day sitting with Josh on the beach, watching him draw, she almost felt like she couldn't breathe. But the thought of being alone, idly wasting time because she didn't know what else to do, depressed her even more.

She turned over and tried to go back to sleep. It was only ten o'clock. She could snooze until eleven, and then have a late breakfast, and then . . . then. . .

With a groan, she got out of bed. The irritable energy coursing through her meant there was no chance of going back to sleep. She had a long shower, and deep-conditioned her hair, and spent ages doing her make-up and choosing her clothes. She was all dressed up with nowhere to go.

"Morning, love," her mother said as she slouched into the kitchen.

Lila grunted, and wrestled two pieces of bread into the toaster with more force than necessary.

Her mother laid down the file she'd been reading. "You're all sweetness and light this morning," she observed. "What's the matter?"

Lila banged open the fridge and stared morosely at the contents.

"Come on, love," said her mother briskly. "Let's have a cup of tea."

Lila wanted to groan. Her mother was a psychotherapist, and who wanted to be psychoanalysed by their own mother? But something sat her down at the kitchen table with her toast as her mother poured out two mugs of tea, slid one mug towards Lila and waited with an enquiring look on her face.

"Don't look at me like that, Mum," she muttered.

Her mother stirred her tea. "Look at you like what?"

"Like you want me to 'talk'."

Her mother smiled. "I *do* want you to talk. And I think you want to talk as well. Otherwise you'd have taken that toast up to your bedroom, wouldn't you?"

Her mother had a point, Lila realized. She wriggled uncomfortably on her chair. "I don't know what's the matter with me," she began. "I'm so restless, I could scream. I'm thinking about the future, and I'm thinking about Josh, and I'm so *bored*—"

Her mother reached across and took her hand. "Why do you think you're feeling like this?"

Lila gestured hopelessly at the kitchen walls. "All

my friends are doing things they like, stuff that will help their futures. They have their lives all mapped out inside their heads, and they're all going to be brilliant at what they do. What do I have? Nothing."

"Josh is hardly nothing," her mother said.

"I don't want to be defined by my boyfriend," Lila said, nettled. "This is the twenty-first century, Mum. And anyway," she added, "I'm having doubts about Josh and me too."

Her mother looked concerned. "What kind of doubts?"

If only they were the kind of doubts she could put into words, thought Lila hopelessly. "He's nice and lovely and kind," she tried, "but we never do anything exciting, we never go anywhere new, we never see things we've never seen before, or . . . anyway, he'll probably meet someone better on his course, someone who's as talented as he is and twice as beautiful as me." That thought pained her more than she could say.

"You *are* in a muddle," said her mother. "On the one hand you say you're bored with Josh, and in the same sentence you're worrying about him meeting someone else."

Lila silently lifted a shoulder in response. Real life *was* a muddle. Nothing was black and white.

"Josh is a lovely boy, Lila," said her mother. "But that's not enough if he doesn't make you happy."

"He does . . . sometimes," Lila groaned, resting her head in her hands. "But then I catch myself snarling at him all the time, and he looks so hurt. . . Maybe I should just end it." It sounded strange and frightening when she said it out loud.

"You're in a rut, that's all," her mother soothed.

That was almost the worst of it. "I'm fifteen years old," said Lila passionately. "My life shouldn't be in a rut already!"

"Here's what you do," said her mother. "You find something new to do. Josh as well. That boy has a lot of good in him."

"You think I don't know that?" Lila demanded.

"Give it a try," said her mother, looking unperturbed. "Find somewhere new that you can go together."

"He's doing his course today," Lila muttered.

"Then let's focus on you." Her mother steepled her fingers, resting her elbows on the table. "You have a lot of different talents, Lila. You were a little dynamo when you were growing up, so full of ideas and imagination. Do you remember how you used to play make-believe for hours in your bedroom with your teddies?"

Lila smiled reluctantly. "I did teddy school on the window sills."

"Not just teddy school. Teddy everything. You built them houses out of bricks and books. You had a naughty one, I remember, what was its name. . ."

Lila had a flash memory of a threadbare black toy cat, all arms and legs and whiskers. "Dodger," she said. How could she have forgotten? "Dodger was the troublemaker."

Her mother laughed. "You were always making him sit in the corner for being naughty in your school games. You wrote stories about him. You even built a jail for him, out of an old box Dad had in the garage."

Even now, Lila could see Dodger's naughty face peeping out through the wonky string bars she'd stuck over a hole in the box she'd turned into her jail. *If only life was still so simple*, she thought wistfully. "That was fun and everything," she said aloud, "but I was seven, Mum. It's kids' stuff."

"That imagination is still going strong," said her mother. "The stories you came out with when you were late for curfew shortly before we left London. . . Dad and I would tear our hair out at you, but we'd have a good laugh in private once we'd sent you up to your room."

Lila flushed, remembering. "I don't do that any more."

"There's a blessing!" said her mother ruefully. "You wrote stories all through primary school, you know. I've still got a few in my desk drawer. Wait there, let's see if I can find any."

Five minutes later, Lila found herself staring at her own childish writing, complete with stick-man illustrations, as her mother pressed a fold of paper into her hands. "*The Adventures of Mr Egg*," she read, laughing and squirming at the same time. "He was a spy."

"How he never got splatted by all the villains and tanks and explosions and dangerous cake-baking exploits, I'll never know," said her mother.

Lila grinned. Mr Egg! His motto had been *Eggstremely Dangerous*. "He had a sixth sense for risk," she said.

Her mother patted her hand. "You should do something with that wild imagination of yours, love. You'll surprise yourself, I guarantee it."

Lila thought about Mr Egg. She thought about Dorothy Watkins and Andrew the cat; Mr Wrinkles and Maria and Hans. She had more stories tucked away in her room upstairs somewhere. She suddenly found herself wanting to dig them out.

Excusing herself from the table, she took the stairs two at a time and dug through several old shoeboxes at the back of her wardrobe. There was a story she'd written once, something she'd been really proud of. . . A rainbow, that was it. A rainbow, and pilots, and a cloud war.

"Got you!" she said, pouncing on a fold of lined paper tucked at the bottom of one of the shoeboxes. She shook out the paper and started reading it. It wasn't too bad, given she'd scrawled it down when she was only twelve. There were even a few decent jokes. It just needed a bit of tweaking. Spreading the paper out on her desk, she sat down and opened her laptop.

It didn't take long to type the story up. She embellished it in a few places, and read it over a few times to double-check the spelling. Then, on a whim, she typed *story competition* into Google and pressed enter.

There were hundreds of competitions. Lila scanned them quickly, trying to find one that would suit. You had to pay to enter some of them, so she avoided those. Some had actual prizes, while others simply promised to publish the winners' stories on their websites.

She suddenly caught sight of a competition called Write a Rainbow. The deadline was the very next day.

If that's not a sign, I don't know what is, she thought, feeling excited.

Before she could change her mind, she scrawled a fake name across the top of her story and pressed *send*. And the moment her story vanished from the screen, Lila found herself wishing she could fetch it back.

TEN

"Your feet stink," Josh remarked.

"They don't," Lila objected.

"When did you last wash them?"

Her boyfriend could be really annoying sometimes. Lila moved her feet a little irritably from his lap, despite being almost too comfortable to move.

The weather had stymied any plans for "doing something different" with Josh today, as her her mum had suggested. *At least we're not on the beach*, Lila thought, gazing out of the living-room window at the rain as it fell in silver sheets from the sky. She rested her head on the sofa cushions and stared at the ceiling for a while.

"Anything interesting up there?" Josh enquired.

"Spiders," Lila replied. "Big ones."

"How big?"

She said the first thing that came into her head. "Big as llamas."

Josh yanked out his sketchbook and flipped to a fresh page. Without even looking, Lila knew he'd be drawing llama-spiders. She wasn't sure she wanted to see how they turned out.

The remote was just out of reach, on the coffee table. Wriggling as far down the sofa as she could, Lila stretched her feet out and took hold of the remote between her toes, successfully dropping it in her lap. She glanced triumphantly at Josh.

"I'm not touching that now your feet have," said Josh, barely looking up from his sketching.

That was fine by Lila. Whenever her brothers got the remote, they played couch commando all evening and she never got to choose what to watch.

"Today we shall mainly be watching . . . daytime TV," she said, pressing buttons haphazardly. "Boring, boring, boring . . . ooh!"

Lorna Lustre's smooth brown face loomed at the camera on the familiar set of *The Blonde Game*. Her eyelashes were so long, they probably wouldn't have looked out of place on Josh's llama-spiders.

"I remember this episode," Lila said, sitting up with interest. "It's when she catches her tennis coach with her best friend. Did you ever see this one?"

Josh was too busy drawing to reply. Lila leaned a little closer to the screen, intrigued by Lorna Lustre's perfectly made-up face. Lila idly wondered how long it had taken to create this look. The reality star's blonde hair hung in perfect frizz-free waves around her face, her skin looked impossibly smooth, and her lips were so puffy and shiny, Lila half-thought she might have suffered an allergic reaction to her lipgloss. She snorted with laughter at the idea.

"What's so funny?" Josh asked, still sketching.

"*The Blonde Game*. Seriously, who hangs out at a tennis club in full make-up, drinking *cocktails*? Lorna Lustre *can't* be her real name. She's so dumb, she makes her tennis racket look intelligent."

Josh's sketchbook slid off his lap and hit the floor as he snatched the remote control out of Lila's hands. "There must be something else on," he said, flipping channels.

Lila tried to snatch the remote back again. "I was *watching* that!"

"You were watching *The Blonde Game*?" Josh said incredulously. "Lila, are you serious? It's a show for idiots. Lorna Lustre sets women's rights back a hundred years every time she minces on to the screen in those ludicrous fluffy high-heeled slipper things."

"She's not wearing fluffy mules today, she's wearing *trainers*," Lila snapped. Dimly she could hear how ridiculous she sounded. "What do you care what I'm watching anyway? You're drawing. You're always drawing. I can watch a hundred episodes of *The Blonde Game* back to back if I want."

Josh snorted. "I can practically hear your brains dribbling out of your ears."

Lila suddenly felt weirdly tearful. Did Josh think she was an idiot? With one final lunge, she got her fingers to the little black box and yanked it from Josh's hand.

"What is your problem?" she demanded. "That show's just a bit of fun. It's not trying to be intellectual or arty or anything like that. It's entertainment."

Josh snatched up his sketchbook again. "I just think it's a low kind of entertainment," he said. "That's all."

He must think I'm really shallow, Lila thought miserably. She didn't even want to watch it now, but there was no way she'd let Josh know that. Making a great show of turning the TV on again, she flicked back to the right channel and stared unseeingly at the screen. It took her a few moments to realize she was staring at an advertisement for hair removal cream.

She felt Josh take her hand.

"I'm sorry," he said quietly. "Let's not fight about something this stupid."

Lila pulled her hand away. "Good to know you think I'm stupid," she said in a brittle voice.

Josh looked upset. "I didn't mean it that way, Lila. Lila!"

Lila flicked the TV off and stalked out of the living room, smarting with humiliation. She headed up to her room and slammed her bedroom door. She knew she was behaving childishly, but it felt good all the same.

He can draw his stupid llama-spiders but I can't watch TV, she thought resentfully. *Double standards or what?*

Her phone buzzed in her pocket.

LILZZZ! Sorry I missed ur text!!
Heading 2 ur beach laterz. Wanna meet up?
xx Iris xx

Her bad mood vanished like fog on a sunny day as she stared at the message in delight. She hit the call button.

"Lost your phone, did you Riz?" she said.

Iris sounded amused. "You know me too well, babes. Left it in the back of Flynn's car. We're driving down later, wanna hang out?"

Lila couldn't think of anything she wanted more. "Who's we?"

"Me, Flynn, Leo, maybe a few others. Supposed to be sunny later."

"I am *so* up for that," said Lila happily. "We could have a party at this secret cove we go to, just east of the main beach. What time are you coming?"

"I need to get Flynn out of bed first. Like the idea of a party, babes. We'll call you, OK? Text us directions."

Lila sent directions the moment Iris hung up, her fingers flying across the keypad. Then she sent a message to all her Heartside friends, telling them there would be a party at the secret cove that afternoon.

Already the rain was fading outside, the sky starting to pick itself out of the grey and turn blue. She wanted to hug herself with excitement. At last, something *different* was happening.

There was a knock at her bedroom door. Her bad mood all but forgotten, Lila beamed as Josh came in.

"Are you OK?" he asked cautiously.

"Never better," said Lila. "Some old mates are coming down from London later. We're going to hang out at the beach, have a party."

"Tonight?" Josh frowned. "That's pretty sudden."

"Iris texted me and it snowballed." She wouldn't let him spoil her unexpected happiness. "It's going to be great. You'll love them, they're all loads of fun. They're going to shake this place up a bit."

Josh sat down on her bed and rubbed his ear. "I thought we were going to the Heartbeat tonight."

"We go to the Heartbeat every night," said Lila, rolling her eyes. Why couldn't Josh be happy for once? "Lighten up, will you? You look like I just invited you to a funeral."

"You might have told me before you started inviting people," he said. "I might have made plans."

Lila felt a sudden rush of anger. "We *always* do stuff you want to do," she snapped. "So tonight, we're doing something for me instead. Just because you're doing your fancy course at the uni doesn't mean you're more important than me!"

"Where did that come from?" Josh protested, looking hurt. "I never said I was more important than you."

Lila wanted to scream. She took several deep breaths to calm herself down. "I'm sorry, I didn't mean that the way it sounded. I just . . . Josh, I really want to do this. OK? Can you at least *try* to enjoy yourself?"

Her phone buzzed four times in swift succession. Iris had clearly been busy spreading the word about the beach party, to judge from the names scrolling up her screen. She hadn't heard from half these guys in months.

Suddenly, Lila started to feel worried. Was mixing old and new friends such a good idea? What if everyone hated each other? She'd changed a lot since leaving London. Maybe they'd changed too.

"It's going to be a great night, Josh," she said. "Trust me."

But she crossed her fingers, just in case.

ELEVEN

The cove was booming with music from Leo's decks, which he'd set up in the shade of the cliffs. There were at least a hundred kids here, Lila estimated, looking around at the mass of faces. She'd dressed in one of her favourite outfits from her London days: a slightly sheer red dress her father had always loudly disapproved of. With her hair tousled to within an inch of its life and the biggest hoop earrings she owned swinging from her ears, she felt more alive than she had in weeks.

The sun had lived up to its earlier promises, and the cove was blazing with sunshine that glinted off the pools of rainwater that had gathered among the rocks.

The dazzling effect made Lila feel like she was dancing among diamonds.

Iris's hair was halfway down her back now, the ends dip-dyed green. With her sharp green eyes outlined in electric-blue mascara, she looked like a wild-eyed mermaid. Lila had so much she wanted to talk to her old friend about, but the music was too loud for much in the way of conversation. Besides, Iris was more of a dancer than a talker.

She was gasping for a drink. Tearing herself away from the dancing, she wandered across the sand to where Josh was perched on a rock.

"Don't you ever put that sketchbook down?" Lila said, swigging from a water bottle. "Josh, it's a party! Come and dance with me."

Ignoring the hand she had playfully extended towards him, Josh eyed the cliffs. "That music's so loud it's going to start a rockfall," he commented.

Lila couldn't help a brief glance at the rockface directly above Leo's decks. Rain was notorious for causing rockfalls along this coast, and there'd been plenty of it that morning. If Leo's music dislodged something, half the party would be crushed in seconds.

"Great," she said, pouting. "You just punctured my party mojo big-time. I hope you're proud of yourself."

"I'm not setting out to puncture anything," Josh said mildly. "I'm just pointing out the obvious."

Lila could feel herself starting to seethe. Ever since the party had started, Josh had been sitting on the rocks and ignoring everyone. It was making her look bad. Even Iris – not famous for noticing much beyond her own enjoyment – had remarked on it.

"I don't think your boyfriend likes the way we smell," she'd said as Leo had started cranking up the volume and the dancing had grown wilder.

Lila had flushed. "He's not into parties."

"He's a right barrel of laughs," Iris had replied. The cat-like gleam in her green eyes had spoken volumes, none of it good.

Iris is right, Lila thought mutinously. *Why does Josh have to be so serious all the time?*

"You're so . . . uptight," she complained now. "We're just having fun. Remember fun?" She waggled her hands in the air, jazz-style.

Josh looked directly into Lila's heavily made-up eyes. "I don't like this kind of fun."

"Why not?"

"You're different when you're with them." He considered her. "And not good different."

Lila felt as if the wind had been knocked out of her. All she was doing was trying to enjoy herself. OK, so she was dressed differently, with different make-up maybe . . . but this was a *party*. Who did Josh think he was?

"Fine," she said through clenched teeth. "Be like that. I don't need you to have fun."

Josh had already returned to his drawing. "I never said you did," he replied.

Lila opened her mouth for a crushing retort, but couldn't think of anything to say. Deciding silence was as effective a weapon as any, she stalked back to Iris and the other dancers.

"Who's been raining on your parade?" asked Iris, amused by the look on Lila's face.

"Shut up and let's dance," Lila grumbled.

They danced as the sun set over the sea. Someone built a large bonfire by the water's edge as the tide crept out, and several dancers relocated to the flames, to cast weird, swaying shadows on the rocks. There were more people now, drawn by the flames and the boom of the music. When a few pebbles rained down on the crowd from the cliffs overhead, Leo moved his decks to a safer spot. The party resumed, louder and wilder than before.

A few partygoers headed for the main beach and the town, seeking out kebabs and fish and chips. When they returned, they seemed to bring twice as many people with them. It was getting difficult to see the sand for the crowd. There was no sign of the Heartside gang. Lila found herself watching the cliff path like a hawk as people poured in from the main beach, beer bottles glinting in their hands.

"Flynn, have you seen Josh?" she shouted.

Flynn flipped his long sweaty dark hair out of his eyes. "Josh who?"

"My— the guy I came to the party with." Something stopped Lila from saying "boyfriend".

"Long gone," said Iris, snaking up with her arms around Flynn's waist. "Find someone else, Lil. He was as boring as a stick. There's plenty of hotties here to choose from."

A panicky feeling settled in Lila's stomach. "Gone?" she repeated. "What, left the party?"

"You mean the lanky dude with the sketch pad?" said Flynn. He'd never been very quick on the uptake. "Yeah, he went. He took the path back to town."

Lila shouldered her way along the path towards the main beach, hunting for Josh's familiar hat, her emotions see-sawing from anger to fear. Why had Josh left?

He's had enough of you, whispered the voice in her head.

"Hey, hi . . . anyone seen a guy with a sketch pad and a hat? Anyone seen a guy with a hat?"

She met blank faces most of the way along the path, but repeated her question doggedly. When she found him, she would. . . She didn't know what she'd do, but it wouldn't be good.

"Hi," she said to a group of girls heading towards her with kebabs in their hands. "Have you seen a tall guy in glasses and a hat?"

"Is he cute?" said one. Her friends laughed.

Josh's electric green eyes twinkled in Lila's head. "Yes," she said, a little reluctantly.

"Saw a cute guy in a hat leaving in a car," offered the tallest girl in the pack.

Lila felt puzzled. Maybe Josh's grandfather had a car. "Who was driving?" she asked.

"She was tall and blonde, is all I know. Nice car too. Red."

Lila felt bewildered. *She?* "Are we talking about the same guy?" she said.

"How would I know?" the girl asked with a shrug. "He was tall, he had a hat. Can we go now?"

Lila bit her lip in vexation as the girls moved on down the path. The guy in the car wouldn't have been Josh, she felt sure of it. He didn't know any blonde girls who drove red cars.

She wandered around the town beach for a while, shivering in her short blue dress. Then she trudged back to the secret cove.

The crowd seemed to have doubled again. Older kids she didn't know were pushing and shoving each other around the bonfire, beer bottles glinting in their hands. Lila tried and failed to spot Iris or Flynn in the crowd. There was no sign of the Heartside High crowd either. Even Leo had vanished. There was a girl in blonde dreads working his decks instead. Judging from the noise, the party was getting out of control.

This was only meant to be a bit of fun, she thought helplessly.

What had she started?

TWELVE

Huddled among the rocks with her arms wrapped tightly around her knees, watching the shouting crowd yelling and laughing, jumping in the sea and climbing the rocks, Lila had never felt so alone. Every time she heard the sound of a smashing bottle, she flinched again.

The secret cove will be covered in broken glass for ever, she thought miserably. *And everyone will hate me for it.* Why had she suggested a party? Why had she idealized her London friends the way that she had?

She of all people should have remembered how Iris never knew when to stop. The party disaster in London had partly been Iris's fault. *I put the invite on Facebook, babes. You don't mind, do you?* Lila *had* minded, a lot. She'd minded even more when the partygoers trashed her parents' house and her dad's job with the police force came under threat because of all the underage drinkers in his home. Flynn went along with anything Iris suggested. Leo . . . she'd hardly even seen him tonight. What strange demon had made her bring all this chaos back into her life?

I wanted to feel more alive, she thought, shivering in the evening wind blowing off the sea. *Now I just wish I was in bed, curled up under my duvet and watching* The Blonde Game *on the TV*. That stupid reality show made her think of Josh, and how he'd left her alone tonight. It made her feel even worse.

I'm lonely, she realized sadly. *How pathetic is that?*

"Hey, party girl," said a familiar voice. "What are you doing curled up in there like a little clam in a shell?"

Ollie was grinning at her over the top of the rocks. Polly was next to him, holding his hand and staring wide-eyed at the party. Becca and Eve, and Rhi and Brody were just behind Ollie and Polly on the path. Lila was so relieved to see them all that she almost burst into tears.

"Thank God you came," she gabbled. She stood up with difficulty. Her legs had cramped from sitting in one place for so long. "Where have you guys *been*?"

"We were at a movie," said Ollie. "We only got your text when we left the cinema. We met this lot on the way over." He frowned at the chaos on the beach. "Did World War Three start without us?"

"Lila, do you know all these people?" asked Polly in awe.

"I don't even know the people I know," Lila said. She was feeling better already.

Polly looked confused. "What?"

"I think she's being ironic," Eve said. She looked distastefully at a couple snogging a few yards from her feet. "Must they do that here?"

"I don't recall you and Max having a problem snogging on this beach," said Ollie.

"He got you there, babes," Becca said, planting a warm kiss on Eve's cheek.

"That was *then*," said Eve with dignity.

Brody struck up on his guitar, singing: "All grown up and nowhere to go . . ." until Rhi silenced him with a kiss.

Lila felt her heart getting lighter as she watched her friends messing around. *This is where I belong,* she thought. *With these guys. They're better mates than Iris, Flynn and Leo ever were.*

"Where's Josh?" Polly asked, glancing around.

The warm, fuzzy feeling in Lila's tummy disappeared. "Not here," she admitted, biting her lip. "He wasn't enjoying the party much."

Someone staggered towards them from the dancing crowd, fell over and was violently sick on the sand.

"I'm not either," said Ollie, wrinkling his nose as Polly shrieked.

The girl on the sand had green-dipped hair. Lila's eyes widened. "Iris?" she said in horror.

Iris's cat eyes focused in recognition. "Lilz," she slurred. "Lilz, babes, not feeling so . . . oops. . ."

"Urgh, she vomited on my *shoes*!" Eve hissed in disgust, trying to leap away from the freshly splattered mess on the sand.

Iris giggled weakly. "I puked on Prada. . . Oopsadaisy. . ."

"She's the drunkest person I've ever seen," said Ollie in fascination.

"I know her," said Lila, embarrassed. "She's drunk too much."

"No kidding, Sherlock," said Polly.

Lila tried to pull Iris to her feet, but it was like trying to make a bag of wet cement stay upright. "Can one of you help me?" she pleaded, looking imploringly at her friends.

Rhi took Brody's guitar and stood well back as Brody leaned down and hefted Iris into his arms.

Iris brushed at her sick-matted hair and fluttered her half-focused eyes at Brody's muscles. "Thanks, gorgeous," she giggled.

"You have vomit on your chin," said Eve with icy disdain. "I'd lose the chat-up lines if I were you."

Iris scrubbed at her face with the back of her hand as Brody set her gently back on her feet. Any minute now and she'd keel over on the sand again.

"You'll be OK with me, Iris," Lila said, trying to keep her old friend upright. "Come on, I'm taking you home."

"You're taking her back to your place?" said Eve incredulously. "What if she throws up on your carpet?"

"I can't leave her out here, can I?" said Lila. "Are you going to help me or what?"

They lifted and shoved, pushed and pulled Iris down the narrow path to the main beach. Everything was going well until Iris had a sudden burst of energy, broke away from them and ran into the sea with a shriek.

"At least the smell's improved," remarked Ollie as they coaxed the now wet and shivering girl back up the beach.

Half an hour later, they had arrived at Lila's front door with Iris supported between them. It was half past midnight and all the lights were out.

"I'll take it from here," Lila whispered. "I'm really sorry about this evening, guys. I love you all. Thanks for bailing me out."

"Tell that to the shoes," growled Eve.

Becca rubbed her back. "They're just shoes," she said.

Polly and Lila exchanged a glance as Eve winced. Brody laughed softly.

"That's like telling Ollie football's just a game," said Rhi.

"I *hate* that," said Ollie.

When her friends had gone, Lila managed to open the front door with her latch key and heave Iris inside. She deposited her on the sofa in the living room, stripping off her wet and stinking clothes and wrapping her in an old blanket she dug out from a box under the stairs. As a precaution, she found a big bucket in the kitchen and set it beside the sofa.

"Love you, babes," Iris mumbled, curling into the blanket. "Sorry for the hassle."

Lila climbed the stairs. She felt weary to her bones.

"I can't say I'm happy about any of this," said Lila's mother, regarding a whey-faced Iris as she sipped weakly at a cup of tea the next morning.

Lila's fingers stank of disinfectant. She tried to hold them as far away from her body as she could. "Sorry, Mum," she said humbly. "But Iris had nowhere else to go and she was in such a state, I couldn't leave her at the beach. It won't happen again."

"We thought you'd left this behaviour in London, Lila," said her father in a sharp voice.

Her dad was being unfair, Lila thought. It wasn't

her who'd thrown up in the downstairs loo. She'd been up since nine, cleaning up the mess. Didn't that show some kind of responsibility? But she knew better than to say anything.

"Sorry, Dad," she said with as much contrition as she could manage.

Her father gave Iris one last disgusted glance and stalked out of the house, slamming the door behind him. Iris gave a groan and pressed her hands to her head.

"I'll take Iris to the train station, Mum," Lila promised. "There's a train for London leaving at ten-thirty."

"You do that." Her mother looked like she was about to say something else, but she kissed Lila on the cheek instead.

The whole way to the station, Iris mumbled jokey apologies, squinting into the sun through her sunglasses. Lila found she was only half-listening. *It was amazing what a difference a few months could make*, she mused.

At the station, Lila found herself on the receiving end of a warm, faintly sick-smelling hug. "Stay in touch, OK?" Iris called, leaning out of the window as the train pulled away. "Missing you already, great evening, babes, let's do it again soon!"

Let's not, Lila thought with a shudder, lifting her hand and waving until Iris was out of sight. A wash of relief came over her.

Sitting down at a bench as the train rounded the corner, Lila pulled out her phone to check for messages. She hadn't heard a thing from Josh since he'd disappeared the night before. They were supposed to be meeting for fish and chips at the beach that afternoon, but Lila found herself wondering whether Josh would even show up.

No messages. She didn't know whether to feel worried or relieved.

Hey, she typed tentatively on her phone. *Still on for lunch today?*

She had bitten three nails before Josh responded.

Sorry, can't make it.
Talk later

Lila felt sick. Josh never cancelled on her. He always put kisses on his texts. Last night had changed something between them.

Maybe he's trying to teach me a lesson, she thought, trying to keep a lid on the feeling of panic roiling in her gut. *Reminding me that I can't take him for granted.*

It was working.

Her phone buzzed again. Lila tapped the screen quickly, hoping for something else from Josh. But instead of a text, a new email was winking in her inbox.

From: fiona@writearainbow.com
To: lilz999@murrayhouse.com
Subject: Writing competition

Lila almost dropped her phone in shock. The writing competition. She'd forgotten all about it. *They were emailing her.*

For one blissful moment, she saw her future. Publication of her story, interviews in the local press, maybe a TV show. A publisher would snatch her up, offer her a six-figure publishing deal over champagne and oysters. . .

Dizzy with imagined glory, Lila opened the email.

Dear Entrant,

Thank you for entering our writing competition.

I'm sorry to tell you that you weren't

successful this time. Keep writing!

Yours sincerely

Fiona Langland

Write a Rainbow

Lila groaned with disappointment and buried her head in her hands.

So much for *that* idea.

THIRTEEN

Lila spent the next morning listlessly poking around the shops, hanging around the pier in the hope of bumping into one of her friends and trying her best not to brood on the disappointment of her rejection email from Write a Rainbow. Clouds had been covering the sun for almost an hour now, spoiling her idea of a day people watching at the beach. She was sitting on the pier, moodily looking at some seagulls as they picked at an abandoned piece of bread, when she got a text from Josh.

> **Come over to mine? 5 Orlop Square. Grandpa will be there. Any time after 1 xx**

The kisses were back, Lila was relieved to see. For a while there, she'd thought. . . But now Josh had messaged her, and she was feeling a hundred times better. Suddenly, there was a plan, and it was just as Josh had promised. She was going to meet his grandfather at last.

She checked her watch eagerly. It was already midday.

Can come now if U want? xxx

Josh's answer came instantly.

Promise not to come before 1 xx

Lila wondered what Josh was doing until one. As far as she knew, the illustration course hadn't suddenly sprouted a Thursday morning class.

Why not?

Just promise.

Lila couldn't be bothered to argue.

Fine, I promise!!! See you after 1 xx

At least it gives me time to get my outfit right, she reminded herself as she sent the text.

She walked back home and spent a happy half hour poking through her wardrobe, trying to decide on an outfit that Josh would like and his grandfather would approve of. Jeans felt too scruffy. Most of her dresses had hems that were a little too short for tea with anyone's grandfather. Lila settled at last on a white shirt dress that Eve must have left at her house. Since Eve was even taller than Lila, it fell to her knees and Lila felt pleased at how respectable she looked. She belted the dress with a thin braided brown belt that Polly had made for her, and brushed her long hair until it shined, before pulling it into a low tidy bun. Slipping on some simple blue ballet flats, Lila examined her reflection in the mirror critically. She didn't normally look quite so polished, and she was pleased with the overall effect. Before grabbing her bag, Lila applied just a touch of brown mascara and some light pink lipgloss. Grandparents never liked much make-up.

Half past twelve. Dawdling through town again, Lila bought herself a sandwich and a drink for lunch and sat on the sea wall for a while. It was hard not to keep constantly checking her watch. Orlop Square, according to her phone, was deep in the warrens of the Old Town, a few twisting streets away from the Heartbeat. As she ate her sandwich, Lila conjured a hundred different scenarios for what she would find.

Josh's grandpa would be in a wheelchair, a blue checked blanket over his skinny knees and the curtains drawn. *"I can't abide the light. . ."* The house would be so tiny that she would have to duck through all the doors, and Orlop Square would be dark and dingy and damp. Josh would greet her at the corner, worried that she would judge him for where he lived. *"Mind the rats, they come up the streets at high tide. . ."*

It was five to one. Lila tried to brush away her nerves as she climbed off the sea wall, studied the map on her phone one more time, and headed for Orlop Square. The sun was starting to come out now, and she was sorry to leave it behind as she turned into the dark, narrow alleys of the Old Town.

The stones were cool here, the roads too narrow for anything bigger than a bicycle. Once or twice, Lila worried that she was lost – until she caught a glimpse of the sea on her left, through a gap in the buildings. She was going the right way after all.

The alley she was in suddenly widened.

She looked around at the little white-painted houses clustered around the cobbled space. An ornate iron water pump stood in the middle, as pretty as a picture.

She walked up to number five and knocked on the sea-green door. A tall man with dark brown hair, a soft flannel shirt and bare feet appeared in the doorway.

"I'm guessing you're Lila. I'm Bill Taylor," he said, and smiled. "Josh is in the garden. Come on through."

Lila could feel herself staring. This guy was Josh's grandfather? *He looks the same age as Dad.*

She followed him through the green door, staring at the pictures that hung on every wall inside the house. All of them were by Josh. She'd have known his style anywhere.

They passed through a wide living area full of pale grey sofas clustered around a large driftwood coffee table topped with glass and scattered with fishing magazines. Fishing rods stood in umbrella stands in almost every corner. The house seemed endless. Lila glanced back at the front door in confusion.

"I didn't expect this place to be so big from the front," she blurted.

"Appearances can be deceptive. This house is three cottages knocked into each other."

They were passing through a wide, white-painted kitchen now with a gleaming skylight and plants hanging in baskets from the ceiling. Lila glimpsed Josh through the wide double doors leading out to the courtyard garden. The garden, at least, was small.

Lila felt her stomach dissolving as Josh hugged her and smiled. Everything was OK. She could hardly speak for relief. She sat in the courtyard garden in a pool of sunshine, holding his hand and staring around at the white-walled space with its climbing pink roses and herbs in pots as Josh's grandfather emerged from the kitchen with a pot of tea and a large fruit cake.

"It's officially too early for this, but I won't tell anyone if you don't," Josh's grandfather said, setting the tea and cake on the table.

Lila took a slice of cake. "It's beautiful here," she said, gazing around. "So peaceful."

"Josh's grandmother and I knocked these cottages through twenty years ago. No one wanted these houses back then. If the council had had its way, the whole of the Old Town would have been demolished and replaced by a shopping centre."

"You're very young to be a grandfather," said Lila. "If you don't mind me saying."

Bill threw his head back and laughed. "That's the nicest thing anyone's said to me in years. You must bring Lila round for tea more often, Josh."

Josh seemed edgy. *He's holding my hand,* Lila reassured herself. It was probably strange for him, bringing someone back here. To her knowledge, none of her friends at school had set foot in this house. She took a sip of tea.

"Are you Josh's mum's dad, or his dad's dad?" she asked.

She felt Josh's hand tense in hers. "I don't like fruit cake," he said. "Do we have any biscuits, Grandpa?"

There you go again, Lila thought as Josh stood up. *Changing the subject*. Her curiosity was well and truly piqued now. She followed Josh's loping strides back into the house.

"Are you ever going to tell me about your parents?" she said as Josh rooted around in the kitchen cupboards for biscuits.

"Nothing to tell," Josh grunted. "They aren't here and Grandpa is. I know we've got chocolate biscuits somewhere. Where did you put the chocolate biscuits we picked up at the supermarket earlier, Grandpa?" he shouted back into the garden.

"Think they're still in the car!" came the answering shout.

"Back in a minute," said Josh, scooping up a set of car keys from the kitchen table.

"Josh—" Lila began, but the front door had banged shut.

What was the big deal about Josh's parents? Were they dead, had they abandoned him? Lila felt restless with the sudden need to know the full story. She looked around the living room, the kitchen, poked her head through a door leading to a spacious downstairs loo with a large driftwood-framed mirror. There were no pictures of anyone that might have been Josh's parents. Just Josh and his grandfather, and lots of Josh's sketches in frames on every inch of wall space.

When she came to the foot of the stairs, Lila glanced back at the courtyard garden. It looked as if Josh's grandfather was on the phone. It's now or never, she thought. Taking the stairs two at a time, she peered around every unlocked door, hunting for . . . something. But it was as if Josh's parents had never existed at all.

When she reached the room at the end of the corridor, she pushed it open cautiously. Even more pictures were hung on these walls. Canvases were stacked in every available inch of space; sketchbooks lay in untidy piles on a desk covered with school books and revision notes. But the thing that held Lila's attention were the piles of shiny boxes covering every square inch of the polished wooden floor.

She picked up the boxes and studied them in astonishment. Video games, consoles, trainers, designer clothes. A brand-new TV, tablets and headphones, music decks. Everything still in its packaging, as fresh as if it had just been picked off a shop shelf.

Holding a console box in one hand and a boxed

tablet in another, Lila sank on to the bed. This was clearly Josh's room. There was no mistaking the sketchbooks, or the canvases. But what was with the boxes? This amounted to thousands of pounds' worth of stuff that kids at school would have given their front teeth for. All unopened. All untouched.

Lila tried to make sense of what she was seeing. Josh wasn't rich. At least, he never *acted* like he was rich. His clothes were old, he was always talking about how expensive his drawing materials were. . .

She thought she knew her boyfriend. Maybe she knew nothing at all.

FOURTEEN

"Wakey-wakey, Lila!"

Lila had been thinking about shiny unopened boxes as she ran her hands along the rails of Polly's upcycled market clothes. She made an effort to focus on her friend. "What?"

Polly put her hands on her hips. "For the benefit of your clogged-up ears, I'll ask for the third time: where's Josh today?"

Why does everyone always ask me that? Lila thought. It was as if she was half a person somehow, not interesting enough by herself.

"Sketching somewhere," she said, forcing a smile on to her face. "He's meeting me on the beach in about an hour. I packed two towels, you'll be pleased to know. Josh has this annoying habit of never bringing his own."

"You two are so cute," Polly said fondly.

Lila had an urge to change the subject. "Do you think this would suit me?" she asked, lifting a high-waisted grey jersey midi skirt from the rail and swirling it around herself.

"Gorgeous," said Polly promptly.

"You would say that," Lila pointed out, half smiling. "You're selling it."

Ollie appeared from the back of the stall, clothes over both arms. "She had to make enough money to fly us to America somehow," he joked.

Lila put the skirt back and settled on a set of pretty bracelets that Polly had made from hardware washers, plaited on to a yellow cord so they chinked against each other. The sound reminded her of the clattering of the halyards on the boats down in the harbour, while the colour of the cord matched the bikini she was wearing under her dress. The sun was hot today, and liable to get hotter. Perfect weather for the beach. She and Josh would lie together and *talk*.

Lila had wanted to ask him about the boxes in

his room yesterday, but her nerve failed her at the last minute. What if he'd stolen them? What if her boyfriend was a master shoplifter?

Put your imagination back in the box, Lila told herself. *There will be a perfectly simple explanation.* And today on the beach, she was determined to get it.

She arrived at the pier five minutes early and waited for him, eyeing the rapidly filling beach. Everyone was flooding to the sea today, pouring through the alleys of the Old Town, clambering over the rocks with heavy beach bags in their arms, setting up barbecues and tents and deckchairs. If Josh was late, they wouldn't get their favourite spot by the pier struts.

Half an hour passed. The sand was now thick with screaming children. Even the less popular spots – those bits right by the water's edge that were always covered in seaweed, and the waspy stretches near the beach bins – were filling up. Lila called Josh for what felt like the hundredth time, but got no answer. She felt hot and frustrated. Where *was* he? She didn't appreciate being stood up on the hottest day of the year.

After ten more minutes, Lila conference-called her girlfriends.

“I need you at the beach, guys,” she pleaded. “Josh has stood me up.”

“That doesn’t sound like Josh,” Rhi said in surprise.

“Are you sure you’re at the right place?” Polly checked.

“We always meet at the pier,” Lila said.

“How adorable,” Eve drawled. “We really are little creatures of habit, aren’t we?”

Lila was in no mood for Eve’s teasing. “Just get here, will you?” she demanded. “The town beach is packed but the secret cove might be better. I’ll see you there, OK?”

Where are you? Waited for nearly an HOUR. Gone to the cove with the others.

Fuming, Lila sent her text to Josh and set off along Marine Parade towards the clock tower and the path to the secret cove, weaving her way through the day tripping crowds with their ice creams and sunglasses and shrimping nets. *If he thinks I’ll waste the whole afternoon waiting for him, he can forget it.*

Just as Lila had hoped, the secret cove was much emptier. With no refreshment stands or toilets, it wasn't popular among young families or the old folks who preferred the deckchairs and the action of the main beach. Day trippers tended not to know about it at all. That just left a few groups of local teenagers, half of them fit-looking boys in brightly coloured shorts and early summer tans that identified them as surfers. In her present mood, that suited Lila just fine.

The others arrived soon after.

"I need a swim," said Polly longingly, setting her pretty floral beach bag down beside Lila's and eyeing the glittering water.

"This isn't the Mediterranean, you know," Eve observed, laying out her towel neatly by the rocks. "And salt water plays havoc with your hair."

"I don't care." Polly kicked off her flip-flops and wriggled out of her beach dress. "Who's coming?"

Two boys walked past with surfboards under their arms.

"We're just enjoying the view," Rhi giggled, setting her hat on her black curls.

One of the boys glanced back. "Keep looking, babe," he grinned at Rhi.

Rhi covered her face as Eve and Lila both laughed. "They weren't supposed to hear that," she squeaked.

Lila felt a rush of recklessness. "Hey!" she called after the surfers. "We like your shorts."

The boys stopped. The one who'd winked at Rhi had big brown eyes that flashed with amusement. "They're occupied at the moment," he said.

"I noticed," Lila smiled.

"Bad girl," Eve murmured as the boys headed on towards the water, their gaze flashing back towards Lila. "What would Josh say?"

"Josh isn't here. He can say what he likes." Lila considered the water and the gleaming brown skin of the surfers as they waded into the sea. "You know what? I might join Polly in the waves after all."

She mussed her hair and adjusted the straps on her yellow bikini. Then she set her shoulders and sauntered into the sea. Josh Taylor wasn't the only boy in the world.

"It's gorgeous in here, Lila!" Polly called, beckoning Lila into the deeper stretches of water around the rocks.

"And it just got gorgeouser!" yelled the brown-eyed surfer, to the intense amusement of his blonder friend.

The water was cold, shocking Lila as she plunged in to twist through the waves like an otter and turn her face up to the sun. Through salt-soaked eyelashes, she kept the surfer boys in her line of sight. The waves weren't great today, but the boys were doing their best. The brown-eyed one even managed to stand up for a while, until he glanced around at Lila and lost his balance. Lila couldn't help bursting into laughter.

"You think it's funny, do you?" challenged the surfer, grinning. He paddled out to where Lila and Polly lay floating on the surface of the sea. "Why don't you give it a go?"

Lila'd been quite good at surfing on a holiday she'd been on with her parents the previous summer, but she saw no reason to tell this guy that.

"What do I do?" she said innocently.

The boy guided her on to his board, his hands lingering a little too long around her waist. "Paddle out until you catch a wave. Then stand up."

"Sounds easy enough," said Lila. "What have I got to lose?"

Polly watched with slightly worried eyes as Lila started paddling. She enjoyed the feeling of the water swishing around her arms and toes. She enjoyed the feeling of the boy's eyes on her as well. Turning the board, she waited until there was a reasonable swell. Then, paddling hard, she managed to catch the top of the wave just as it curled over.

Hold the board firmly, jump up, turn sideways. She almost lost her balance, but righted herself at the last minute. "Whoo!" she shouted, shortly before the board hit the sand and she tumbled off, landing head over heels at the boy's feet.

"Was that your first time?" he said disbelievingly.

Lila stood up, brushing at the sand. "Told you it was easy," she said with a shrug.

He suddenly put his arms around her, scooping her off the sand.

"You need to wash that sand off before it gets in your bikini," he informed her, striding out into the waves.

Lila squealed and laughed, pummelling at his arms. "Don't dump me . . . no. . ."

"What the *hell* are you doing with my girlfriend?"

The surfer swung round, coming nose to nose with Josh striding through the waves towards them. Lila gaped at the expression on Josh's face. He looked seriously mad.

"Giving her a bath, mate," said the boy, laughing. "She's a little bit sandy."

Josh poked the surfer hard in the chest. "Put her down. Now."

Lila was starting to feel a little bit stupid, dangling in the surfer's arms like a child between the two boys.

Josh's eyes sparked with anger. "Put. Her. Down," he repeated.

"Are you going to make me?" the boy enquired.

Josh shoved the surfer hard in the chest, making him stagger backwards into an oncoming wave. Lila screamed as she was dumped unceremoniously into the sea so that she came up gasping with seawater in her nose and her eyes stinging with salt. She stared in disbelief at Josh, wrestling in the surf with the other boy.

Her mild-mannered boyfriend appeared to have got himself into a fight.

Over her.

FIFTEEN

"Josh!" Lila shouted, staggering to her feet. "Stop it!"

The surfer was spitting seawater everywhere as Josh barrelled him down in the water for a third time. "Are you crazy?" he was yelling, scrambling to get away. "Get *off* me, you nutcase!"

The water was heavy around Lila's legs, hampering her progress as she waded towards the fight. "Stop it!" she shouted, grabbing Josh's soaking wet T-shirt and attempting to haul him upright. "Josh, *look* at yourself! What are you doing?"

Josh shoved the surfer one last time. Shaking Lila's hand off, he stalked out of the sea, his glasses blurred and splattered with seawater. Lila had the presence of mind to snatch up his hat as it threatened to float out to sea, and waded after him.

"Josh, what was *that* about?" she demanded, finally freeing herself from the water and breaking into a jog to keep up with him across the sand.

Josh spun around so quickly Lila cannoned into him. His green eyes spat fire. "What were you doing with that guy?" he said angrily.

Refusing to be cowed, Lila folded her arms and glared at him. "You stood me up!" she said angrily. "That gives you no right to question what I do."

"I didn't do it on purpose!"

Lila glared harder. "You could have *messaged* me or something! I was standing there like a lemon, wasting the day and boiling to death. Where were you?"

His eyes flickered. "Busy."

"Busy doing what?"

"Something important."

"What is it with you and mystery, Josh?" Lila demanded. "Do you think it's endearing? Well, I've got news for you. It's not. It's just annoying! You don't talk to me, you don't explain things. I saw the packages in your room," she flung at him, glad at the way he flinched. "Where did they come from? Where are your parents, Josh? Who are you, exactly?"

Josh was breathing hard. "I couldn't get away any sooner, OK? I'm sorry I didn't message you but I couldn't help it. It would be nice if you could just trust me."

It was almost laughable. "Why should I trust you?" Lila practically shouted. "You don't trust me!"

Josh pointed at her. "You were flirting with that guy."

"So what if I was?"

"Lila, you're my *girlfriend*. How do you think it makes me feel, seeing you in some other guy's arms?"

"Why should I care how you feel?" Lila said defiantly. "You don't care about me."

Hurt raced across Josh's face like a storm cloud. Lila knew she was behaving badly. This was all too weird. The rules of normal Josh-Lila interaction seemed to be up in the air.

"I don't care about you?" Josh repeated. "Is that what you think?"

Lila wanted to stamp her foot. "What am I supposed to do when you don't show up? I was looking forward to being on the beach with you, and you were off – doing whatever you were doing! I hope it was worth it."

"It wasn't. But what do you care?"

Lila blinked. She had no idea what to say to that.

"I'm not a game player, Lila," Josh said evenly. "I thought things were going well between us. Have I misunderstood something here?"

"Yes . . . no. . . I don't know!" Lila spluttered.

"I don't have time for riddles," he said, rubbing his face. "But I know this. I don't do drama, and I won't be played. Go and have fun with your surfer boys. I'm giving you permission." He gave an awkward bow. "You're free to go."

Lila gaped at him. OK, so she *had* been trying to make him jealous. She *had* been hoping he might show up and see her in the surf with another guy. But this . . . this had got out of hand. Never in a million years did she think he'd *dump* her.

"You're *breaking up* with me?" she said in disbelief.

There was something unreachable about Josh's expression as he plucked his sopping wet hat from between her fingers. His face was closing down, even as she watched. She was thrown back to her first week in Heartside High, her first stilted conversations with a boy she wondered if she'd ever get to know.

"Fine," she managed. "If that's what you want. I never did live up to your expectations, did I? Well, I hope it doesn't get lonely up there on your moral high ground, Josh!"

"I won't be made a fool of," he snarled. Scooping up his bag where he'd dropped it on the sand and cramming his wet hat on his head, he walked away from her.

Lila stayed where she was for a full two minutes, in case he returned and swept her into his arms and told her she hadn't heard him right. Of course he hadn't dumped her. This was all some weird misunderstanding.

Come back, she prayed.

He didn't.

"Fine," Lila said out loud, to no one. "I wanted my freedom anyway."

She had wanted it, hadn't she? So why did it taste so sour in her mouth?

She walked back a little unsteadily to where Eve, Rhi and Polly had all gathered wide-eyed by the rocks.

"Did Josh actually fight that surfer?" Rhi asked in awe.

"He looked like he wanted to drown him," Eve remarked.

Polly gazed at Lila with troubled eyes. "Is . . . everything OK with you guys?"

"No," said Lila. Her voice sounded weird, as if she'd never heard herself talking before. Like she was hovering above the beach, watching herself. "We just broke up."

Polly gasped. Rhi's mouth dropped open. Even Eve, who was normally so hard to surprise, seemed shocked. "Over that little *surfer*?" she said incredulously.

"You were messing around for a grand total of five minutes!" Rhi said in horror.

I won't cry, Lila thought. "Five minutes too long, clearly," she said.

"Josh didn't mean it, whatever he said to you," said Polly. She looked close to tears. "He's crazy about you, Lila. He wouldn't dump you over something like this."

Lila spread her hands. "What do you want me to say? This is all a dream?" *If only.* "Josh and I split up, OK? End of subject."

Her friends exchanged troubled glances. Trying to ignore them, Lila jammed her sunglasses on her nose and lay down stiffly on her towel. Even the sun felt colder than it had five minutes ago.

"Lila, are you OK?" Rhi said after a moment.

"Of *course* she's not," Eve said with an irritated sigh. "You only have to look at her lying there like a motionless corpse to know that. Her boyfriend dumped her over a bit of flirting with a *surfer*. The world has gone mad."

"Lila?" said Polly tentatively. "We'll listen if you need to talk about this."

The sand is too hard right here, Lila thought distractedly. She should have chosen somewhere further up the beach, away from the tideline. She squeezed her eyes tightly shut. *I won't cry, I won't cry, I won't cry.*

"I don't need to talk about anything," she said. "I just want to enjoy the sunshine. Why is everyone being so serious about this? People break up all the time. I'm over it already."

This was turning into the worst summer ever.

SIXTEEN

Lila wished her friends would stop treating her like she was made of bone china. Polly in particular wouldn't stop asking if she was all right. "Fine," she'd said, more times than she cared to count that morning. "I'm fine."

The high street was particularly busy as it was a Saturday. The combination of the weekend and the sunshine had brought people out in droves, bags at the ready, all trying to fit in a bit of shopping before popping down to the beach to carry on where they'd left off the day before, surfing and swimming, building sandcastles and eating ice cream. Lila found she'd gone off the idea of surfing. Even the boys making their way down to the beach with their boards made her turn away and stare at the pavement.

"Are you *sure* you're OK?" Polly said anxiously, squeezing Lila's arm.

"Give it a rest, Polly," said Eve, rolling her eyes. "Can't you see Lila doesn't want to talk about it?"

"She needs cake," Rhi put in. "Let's go to the Ciao Café and sit on the pavement and watch the scenery."

Lila trailed after her friends, letting them order drinks and food and fuss around her. Polly was doing her best to bite her tongue, she could see. She felt grateful to Eve.

She didn't *want* to think about Josh. But ever since yesterday, she'd been unable to think about anything else. She'd been so stupid, behaving the way she had with the surfer. She'd acted like that in London so often, but she wasn't that person any more. Josh had helped her to become someone nicer. Someone calmer, more focused and less inclined to make stupid decisions. She thought she'd worked that out, the night of the disastrous cove party. Now she'd gone and done it again, and Josh had dumped her.

He's so great, she thought, tears blurring her eyes as she sipped at the frappé Eve had bought her. *It's not his fault I'm such a mess. What was I trying to prove by flirting with that guy?*

She was jealous, she realized numbly. Josh knew what to do with his life, and was already so good at it. She wanted that certainty. But because she couldn't see her future, she was going out of her way to ruin everything that was good about her present. *I may not be able to draw or design things, or play football or the guitar or organize parties, but I can flirt like a champion.* She grimaced over her frappé. *Great career choice, Lila. Really terrific.*

It was only now that she'd lost Josh that she fully realized what she'd had. Polly's words echoed mockingly in her head. *Some people don't know what they have until it's gone.*

After their frappés, Eve wanted to try on some clothes in a boutique that had opened recently by the harbour. Lila sat and watched as her friends flitted between changing rooms, laughing and offering opinions, gasping and shaking their heads.

"Not trying anything on?" said Rhi.

Lila shook her head. "I don't need anything, really."

"None of us *need* this stuff," Eve said, stroking

a gorgeous dress in dark green with tiny white dots along the bottom hem. "But it doesn't stop us *wanting* it."

When the others were all in the changing rooms, Lila slipped outside. Standing in a puddle of sunlight on the edge of the road, she took out her phone, willing there to be a message from Josh. The screen was stubbornly blank.

It took her a while to compose exactly what she wanted to say.

I'm really sorry for behaving like an idiot yesterday.
You were right to dump me, although I wish you hadn't.
Forgive me?
Lila xx

She bit her lip, rereading what she'd written. Did she sound too needy? Should she reword the bit about him dumping her?

Send it, she ordered herself.

There was a squeal of brakes as her thumb came

down towards the send button. Lila glanced up to see Josh in the passenger seat of a red sports car as it shot past, a blonde girl in sunglasses at the wheel.

No sooner had she blinked than the car had disappeared around a bend in the road and she was left to question her own eyesight. It had been Josh, she was sure of it. She'd only glimpsed the back of the girl's head, but she'd definitely been blonde, and she'd definitely been driving.

She was tall and blonde, is all I know. Nice car too. Red. That girl at the beach had seen a boy in a car on the night of the party that matched Josh's description. Lila had dismissed it, but all of a sudden the ground felt a whole lot less certain under her feet.

Who was the blonde?

Josh hadn't turned round as they had driven past. He had either failed to spot Lila on the kerb with her head bent over her phone, or he had ignored her on purpose.

Who was she?

Snakes writhed in Lila's belly. Was Josh trying to make her jealous? Give her a taste of her own medicine? If so, it was working.

She stared back at the text she'd been about to send. After a moment's hesitation, she deleted it and stuffed her phone in her bag. No way was she sending it now.

"What happened?" said Polly at once as Lila walked slowly back into the shop. "Where did you go? Is everything OK?"

"I just saw Josh," Lila said.

Eve put her head out of the changing room. "And?"

"He was in a car with some blonde."

Rhi frowned. "Are you sure it was him?"

Lila wasn't sure of much just then, but she *was* sure about that. She nodded.

"Could he have a new girlfriend?" Eve asked. "What?" she protested, raising her hands as Rhi and Polly glared at her. "I'm just voicing the possibility, OK?"

"We only just broke up!" Lila said, horrified. If Josh *had* found someone else, what did that make her? The most forgettable girlfriend ever?

"Have you seen him with this girl before?" Rhi put in.

"Someone saw him with her the night of the party," Lila whispered. "He was getting into her car."

"O. M. *G*," said Polly faintly.

Lila felt as if her entire world was crumbling. Josh had met someone on his illustration course, just as she'd feared. Someone beautiful. Older and rich, too, judging from the car. He must have been seeing her behind Lila's back. *Promise not to come before one*. . .

"What am I going to do?" Lila wailed. She could feel her eyes filling with tears.

"You're going to do nothing," said Eve at once. "Play it cool. Boys hate it when you chase after them. He loves you, Lila. He'll come back in his own time."

"No," Rhi said hotly. "Lila, you have to fight for him. Go after him, ask him outright about this blonde girl. Otherwise you'll lose him for good!"

Lila threw up her hands in frustration. "Do nothing, or do everything. Doesn't anyone have a suggestion in the middle?"

"Give him some space," Polly said. "Maybe he needs to stretch his wings a bit."

Lila had never known anyone happier in their own skin than Josh. He didn't need to run with any crowd, or challenge himself to prove a point, or *date other girls apart from her.* "Josh is not a wing-stretching kind of guy," she said.

"How do you know?" Eve enquired.

"I just do," Lila said stubbornly.

But the old doubts were resurfacing. She thought about the unexplained packages in his room again, and his refusal to talk about his life. She thought she'd known him, but now. . .

"I need to talk to his grandfather," she said suddenly. "See you guys later."

Josh's grandfather will have the answers, she thought, hurrying along the street towards the Old Town. *I'll go round and ask if he knows about this blonde girl.* It would be an embarrassing conversation, but Lila was beyond embarrassment. All she knew what that if she didn't find out what was going on with Josh, she would explode with frustration.

She raced through the narrow twists and turns of the Old Town, finding the route she'd taken on Thursday by pure instinct. She flew into Orlop Square, breathless and determined. She would just knock on the door and ask. Outright. How hard could it—

Lila felt her legs turn to water beneath her. Parked outside the partially open sea-green door of 5 Orlop Square was the red sports car she'd seen half an hour earlier.

In that moment, Lila realized Josh was worth fighting for. It was time. Win or lose. She had to at least try.

SEVENTEEN

The front door stood slightly ajar. Before she could talk herself out of what she was doing, Lila burst through into the brightly lit living room with its pale grey sofas and driftwood table, sending the door banging backwards, hard against the wall.

Josh's grandfather looked round, startled. Josh leaped out of the sofa. The blonde woman stayed exactly where she was, her long tanned legs crossed and ending in the highest pair of black stilettos Lila'd ever seen.

"Lila?" Josh looked utterly horrified. "What are you doing here?"

"This is a pleasant surprise," Josh's grandfather remarked. He reached over to the pot of tea on the driftwood table. "Would you like a cup?"

Lorna Lustre's trademark sunglasses sat on the table beside the teapot, her wide blue eyes framed in familiar layers of thick black mascara. She gazed at Lila with a interested look on her heavily made-up face.

"Hello, you pretty little thing," she said, in that famous husky voice that people loved so much to imitate.

Nothing here made sense.

"You're Lorna Lustre," Lila managed. Lorna Lustre the star of the show *The Blonde Game*, the reality TV show that Josh hated so much.

Lorna Lustre crinkled her nose. "Aren't you a darling girl to know who I am? Are you joining us for tea? Josh darling, take over from your grandfather and play the host. Pour this adorable child a cup of tea."

Josh's face turned as pink as the cushion covers as Lorna Lustre took his hand and kissed it before pushing him gently towards the teapot.

The strange paralysis that had descended on Lila fizzled away, leaving pure jealous rage in its place. Lorna Lustre wasn't allowed to call her a child. Lorna Lustre *definitely* wasn't allowed to kiss Josh's hand.

"Don't you *dare* call my boyfriend 'darling'," she hissed. "And you can stop pawing him as well."

Lorna Lustre threw her head back and laughed. Her perfect blonde curls bounced on her shoulders like a shampoo advertisement. "Young love," she sighed. "There's nothing like it."

"Lila," said Josh in an agony of embarrassment. "This isn't what—"

Lila was too angry to care what she said now. "*Young* love," she snarled at the reality TV star. "The clue's in the name, or hadn't you heard? You're chasing a boy half your age and it's disgusting. You've made a career out of stupidity, but this – this is beyond stupid. It's *pathetic*!"

Josh sank back on to the sofa with his head in his hands. Josh's grandfather simply looked amused as he drank his tea. If anything, Lorna Lustre looked even more delighted.

"Josh, this girl is heaven," she gasped. "Such a breath of fresh air to meet someone with true fighting spirit. Love is worth any battle, darling, I quite agree."

Lila felt her hands curling into claws, ready to scratch. *I will fight you for him,* she thought in a haze of fury. *Don't think I won't.* Pure outrage drove her on. "You must be really desperate, Miss Lustre. Is your TV show in trouble? Are you trying this 'young love' thing to get your ratings up? Is that it?" She looked around warily. "Where have you hidden your cameras?"

"Lila, please stop," Josh begged.

Lila rounded on him. "You're not stupid, Josh. How have you been suckered by this reality-TV vampire? I know she's glamorous and famous and it's probably really flattering being chased by her, but seriously? You dumped me to go out with a Z-list celebrity old enough to be your *mother*?"

Josh groaned and buried his head in his hands again.

"Josh has told me so much about you, Lila." The reality star took a sip of her tea, leaving a smudge of red lipstick on the rim. "It's such a pleasure to meet you at last."

"Well Josh has told me *nothing* about you," Lila shot back. "Then again, he doesn't have to, does he? The gossip mags have done it for him. Your reputation precedes you! I don't care how famous you are. Josh is *mine*."

"The way I heard it," Lorna remarked, "he isn't any more. Something about a surfer? Such a shame."

"That ... that's none of your business!" Lila spluttered. Josh had told this woman what an idiot she'd been? How . . . what. . . ? She could almost hear the conversation. *There there, Josh, young girls can be so cruel. . . Let me kiss your broken heart all better. . .*

Josh had turned an even brighter shade of pink. He couldn't meet her eye. *You're free to go. . . I won't be played. . .*

"That was a *mistake*," Lila shouted, trying to shake the horrible memory from her head. "My mistake, OK, but I know how stupid I was and. . ." Why was she saying all this? *It's a trick*, she thought wildly. *Lorna Lustre knows exactly how to pry out a person's emotions and lay them bare for everyone on TV to see.*

"Put the poor girl out of her misery, Louise," said Josh's grandfather unexpectedly. "Before she starts tearing down my house."

"You're such a spoilsport, Dad," Lorna Lustre pouted. "Things were just getting interesting. Lila and I were having such fun."

Once again, Lila felt the ground shift beneath her feet. Louise? *Dad?*

"I'm not going after Josh, as you would have it, Lila," the reality star sighed. "We go way back, you know. Him and me. Right to birth, in fact." She smiled happily. "I'm Josh's mother, darling. How do you do? I know we're going to be the best of friends."

EIGHTEEN

Lila was struck dumb with mortification as Lorna Lustre's words hit home. She didn't dare look sideways at Josh, who had now buried his entire head in one of the cushions.

Josh's grandfather cleared his throat. "More tea, anyone?"

"You're Josh's *what*?" Lila croaked, unable to tear her eyes away from the woman on the grey sofa.

Lorna Lustre took another sip of tea. "Mother," she repeated. "As in, I gave birth to Josh." She laughed coyly. "I know what you're going to say, darling. I look far too young to have had a boy so big and grown-up. It's terribly sweet of you to think so, but I can assure you, it's perfectly true."

This felt like a storyline in *The Blonde Game*. It couldn't be real. Lila looked beseechingly in the direction of Josh's grandfather. *Tell me this is all a terrible dream.* The older man was halfway towards the kitchen with the teapot in his hand. Making a discreet exit.

If only she could make a discreet exit as well.

She had called Josh's mother disgusting, pathetic and stupid. She'd accused her of seducing her own son. In a state of a thousand agonies, Lila looked one last desperate time at Josh for rescue. He had emerged from the cushion and was now looking at her cautiously, his green eyes dark and anxious.

"I was going to tell you," he said.

Lila gave a little moan of horror and whirled for the door. She had to leave. She had to get away from this nightmare.

"Lila!" she heard as she skidded through Orlop Square, racing for the first cobbled turning she could see. "Lila, come back!"

Josh was giving chase. She could hear his footsteps behind her. Lila put her head down and kept running. If only she could outrun the things she'd said. She'd ruined *everything*.

"Lila, *please* come back!" Josh shouted. "We have to talk about this!"

Lila ran faster, skidding on the smooth cobbles as she took a twisting flight of steps three at a time. She turned right, then right again, trying to lose Josh. She had no idea where she was going. At the rate she was sprinting, she was going to break an ankle, but she didn't care. She had to put as much distance between herself and Orlop Square as she could.

"OH!"

She had cannoned right into Josh, who had suddenly stepped out from an alley she had completely failed to see. He caught her firmly by the arm, to stop her running any further.

"When you live in this place, you get to know the short cuts," he said.

"Let me go," Lila wept, struggling to free herself.

"Keep running this way and you'll run straight into the sea. This street ends in a jetty Grandpa uses when he goes fishing."

The way she was feeling right now, Lila decided the sea was probably the best place for her. "Let me go," she said again, more forlornly.

"Not until you listen." There was a sudden flash of amusement in his eyes. "I never knew you felt so strongly about me."

"Don't laugh at me," Lila shouted, bursting into tears. "I just made a total idiot of myself in front of your mother. Do you have any idea how that feels?"

"Mum can take it. You don't get to be Lorna Lustre without growing a very tough skin."

Lila's legs felt wobbly. She wouldn't have been able to run any further even if she'd wanted to. Standing back, Josh let her slide downwards until she landed with a thump on the shiny cobbles, dashed the tears from her burning eyes and buried her head in her arms. *This is what an ostrich does*, she thought stupidly. *Only they use sand.*

Josh sat next to her. "Mum had me when she was sixteen. Dad wasn't much older. They met on another reality show, something called *Secret Island*. You won't remember it, they haven't rerun it in years, but essentially they put a bunch of teenagers on an island in the middle of the Pacific and watched as they went crazy for the benefit of the viewers." There was a thread of steel in his voice. "Grandpa tried to talk Mum out of going, but she was determined to be famous. My dad was in the same mould. If anything, he was more hungry for it than she was. They fell in love on screen and Mum got pregnant." Josh gave a thin smile. "The viewers loved it. I am the ultimate child of reality TV."

The name of the show rang a bell somewhere deep in Lila's whirring mind. She'd read a hundred articles about Lorna Lustre in the gossip mags. She remembered early pictures of the reality star in a tiny bikini beneath a palm tree. *Secret Island*: the start of Lorna Lustre's career. The start of Josh.

"What happened to your dad?" she found herself asking.

"He was even less capable of rearing a child than my mum. They thought it would be easy, like it was on TV. A smiling baby, cute outfits."

They were only sixteen, Lila thought. *Hardly older than us.*

"Funnily enough, reality was a terrible shock," Josh went on drily. "Grandpa took me on when Mum couldn't cope. Dad left for America around the same time, seeking fame and fortune on the other side of the Atlantic. Last I heard, he'd got a gig on an American soap called *Alpha Mail*. It's about a postman."

Part of Lila wanted to giggle. Most of her wanted to cry. She put her hand tentatively on Josh's arm. "I'm sorry," she said. "I didn't know."

"Why would you?" he said. "I never told anyone. Mum would show up in Orlop Square every once in a while to play at being a parent. Last week, she got in touch after almost a year. Buying me presents, you know, those boxes you saw? But she seemed to have changed. She said she wanted a real relationship with me. And she's my mum after all. . ."

Josh looked tired.

He continued. "This never used to be a problem because I wasn't going out with anyone, I didn't have any friends – I didn't have to tell anyone about my life if I didn't want to. It was different this time." He looked at her. "There was you."

Lila flushed. "You told her we broke up," she said.

Josh grimaced. "I'm a hopeless liar. She asked me if I had a girlfriend last week. I told her about you. Then I told her we broke up. Maybe I thought it would make me more interesting."

Lila took his hand. "You *are* interesting," she said

honestly. "You're the most interesting boy I know."

Josh didn't push her hand away. "I didn't want you to know about my mum, even though she knew about you," he admitted. "I was embarrassed. Your family is so perfect. Mine is a screw-up."

Lila was surprised at Josh's description of her family. "Perfect" wasn't a word she'd have chosen to describe the chaos of her brothers. She opened her mouth to say as much.

"Darling, you're too harsh," said a voice above them. "Every family has its challenges."

Lorna Lustre was standing at the top of the cobbled steps looking down at them on the cobbles, her hands on her slim hips and her sunglasses on her nose. It was the perfect pose, like something out of a film. Lorna Lustre probably did everything with a view to it being filmable. Lila got to her feet awkwardly.

"I'm really sorry I went off at you like that," she made herself say. "It was rude of me. I didn't understand."

Lorna flapped a perfectly manicured hand at her. "Give yourself a break, darling girl. I've heard worse. The tabloids rip me apart at least once a week. I'd rather people had a bad opinion of me than no opinion at all." The reality star gazed at Josh, who was still sitting on the cobbles. "Why don't you both come back to the house? I have to leave this evening, but before I go I have the *most* exciting news."

Josh stood up. "You can tell us out here, can't you?"

Lorna clapped her hands like a little girl. "Well, if you insist," she giggled. "I've got a wonderful opportunity for you, Josh darling. You won't be able to turn it down."

"Try me," said Josh.

Lorna Lustre continued as if Josh hadn't spoken. "And if by some strange twist of fate you *do* turn it down, your lovely Lila will, I'm sure, talk sense into you. She seems like a girl with a sensible head on her shoulders."

Shows how much you know, Lila thought.

Lorna pushed her sunglasses up on her head and fixed Josh with her bright blue stare. "Darling, you're going to be very rich," she said brightly. "I've come down to offer you a spot on my show as my young and handsome son. You're going to be a total surprise to the viewers. No one's seen you since you were a baby. I couldn't have designed it better myself. The ratings will hit the roof the moment you appear.

"Isn't it simply *marvellous*?"

NINETEEN

"I know it's a bit of a shock," Lorna was saying as she looped her arm through the crook of Josh's elbow, "but my producers were on it like a shot when I suggested it. It has *everything*: truth, drama, honesty. We need to discuss the details with your grandfather and talk about contracts of course. We are talking about a *lot* of money, darling, even before the interviews and endorsements start. My agent is offering a very reasonable deal to promote you. He's quite brilliant. He's kept me at the top for over fifteen years."

Lila walked silently behind the TV star as she propelled her son along the cobbles, talking excitedly about her plans all the way back towards Orlop Square.

Josh's grandfather was on one of the sofas when they returned. "Welcome back, Lila," he said. "I hope my daughter has been gentle with you."

Lila flushed and sank miserably on to the sofa across from him. Lorna Lustre clapped her hands.

"I've told him, Dad," she said happily. "And he's absolutely thrilled."

Josh's grandfather's expression didn't change. "Whatever is your mother talking about now, Josh?" he said.

"Dad, I *explained* it all to you last week," Lorna said. "The TV deal? Honestly, you have a brain like those smelly fishing nets you love so much."

Josh didn't look as thrilled as Lorna was suggesting. In fact, Lila thought he looked like he had been carved from stone.

"I suppose it could showcase your art, Josh . . ." she said reluctantly, to fill the silence more than anything.

"Absolutely," said Lorna, nodding. "I knew you were a sensible girl, Lila. We could have a few of your little paintings dotted about on the set."

"I draw," said Josh quietly. "I don't paint."

Lorna was rummaging in her large red handbag. "That gives me a wonderful idea for an episode," she said, drawing out a tablet and typing swiftly with her long red nails. "I have no idea how talented you are at painting, and you surprise me with a gorgeous portrait you've painted without me even noticing. I would of course pose for you off-camera, give you plenty of time to get me in my best light. But the audience doesn't need to know that. It would be the most marvellous surprise!"

Lila frowned. Hadn't she heard her son say that he didn't paint?

Josh's grandfather stood up. "I didn't think you could disappoint me any more, Louise," he said coldly. "It seems that I was wrong."

"Whatever are you talking about, Dad?" Lorna Lustre sounded impatient. "Don't you see what an incredible opportunity I'm offering my son?"

Josh had been staring at his hands for the past few minutes. He looked up now. "Get out of my house," he said.

The smile dropped off Lorna Lustre's face. "I beg your pardon?"

Lila pressed herself back into the sofa as Josh stood up. "I said, get out," he repeated more loudly.

Lorna looked at Lila. "This is what I was afraid of," she said with a pout. "Josh can be as stubborn as a donkey. Talk to him, darling girl. He'll listen to you."

"He won't," said Josh's grandfather. "If you knew the first thing about your son, you'd know that Louise."

Lorna Lustre snatched up her bag and stood up, teetering slightly on her bright blue heels. The laughter had gone from her face. All of a sudden, her eyes looked as hard as sapphires. "Is that all the gratitude I get? It took me *weeks* to arrange this—"

"GET. OUT." Josh howled the words.

Lorna marched to the front door, and turned in the doorway. "You'll regret this," she said, pointing with one long red fingernail. And then the door slammed and she was gone.

"Please forgive my daughter," said Josh's grandfather in the shocked silence that followed the sound of the red sports car squealing away from the cobbles outside. "She scripts her whole life like a soap opera."

Josh had gone out into the courtyard garden, his entire body radiating tension and hurt. Lila followed him, wondering what she could say to make him feel better.

"It's always nice when your own mother arranges for you to re-enter her life as a PR stunt," Josh said, studying the roses that climbed the white courtyard walls.

Lila put her hand on his arm. "I'm really sorry." There wasn't much else to say.

"I had hoped she'd changed. For a while this time, I really thought she was interested in getting to know me."

"Maybe she still is."

Josh snorted. "My mother is one of the most selfish people you'll ever meet. I'm not going to hold my breath."

In a flash, Lila realized why Josh withdrew into his shell whenever she played games, or did stupid things for the sake of attention. It reminded him of his mother.

“I never meant to take you for granted,” he said, glancing at her. “I’m sorry. I got too comfortable in our relationship, I think.”

“I’m sorry too,” she said, feeling a flutter in her stomach. “I’ve behaved so badly. I’ve been blaming you because you know what you want to do with your life, and I don’t. I’m so scared that I’ll never work it out.”

He took her hand, stroking her fingers and listening. It felt nice.

“I have to have something for myself,” Lila said. “I can’t just be someone’s girlfriend.” *Even someone as lovely as you.*

“You’ll work it out,” he said. “I know you will.”

“Can we. . .” Lila began. She stopped, not sure how to continue.

“. . .Try again?” he enquired.

The thought was like a warm bath. Lila smiled at him hopefully.

“You once made a deal with me,” he said, smiling back. “I’d help you focus on your future, and you’d help me loosen up.”

Lila nodded. She remembered everything she and Josh had ever said to each other.

"Lila Murray," he said, taking both her hands this time. "Will you go on a date with me next Saturday?"

Play it cool. Tease him. Make him ask again. . .

"Yes," she said, deliberately ignoring the whispers of her mind. "I'd love to."

TWENTY

Lila paced up and down her room, alternately checking her watch and her reflection. Josh had said he'd pick her up at six. *Ten minutes to go.*

She'd persuaded her mother to take her out for a cut and blow-dry that morning. Her mother had been surprised at first, remembering the fights she and Lila used to have in London about her out-of-control hair. Her mum had always wanted her to keep it under control, but Lila had refused to even try to tame it. "Are you sure, love?" her mum asked probingly. "This doesn't sound like you."

Lila had grabbed her mother's hand and squeezed, hard. "Please? I *really* want to make a good impression tonight."

Her mother's face had softened. "Josh loves you just the way you are," she said, cupping Lila's cheeks in her hands.

Lila wanted to believe that so badly. She was stupidly nervous. *This is Josh*, she had told herself over and over again. *He's seen you with sand in your hair and seawater streaking your mascara. Why does this matter so much?* But it did, and that was that.

"Please?" she'd repeated.

So here she was, her hair shining like a shampoo ad, brushed and swept away from her face in a thick brunette curtain. The last time she'd got a blow-dry had been with Eve in London. That felt like a hundred years ago.

She'd taken extra care with her make-up too, thinking about Lorna Lustre's thick foundation and red lips as she dabbed on a little tinted moisturiser and applied some soft peach eyeshadow to her lids. She was determined not to remind Josh of his mother for even one second tonight.

It was lovely to be wearing the dress Eve had bought her in London again. It was the prettiest thing she owned, short and shimmery and a perfect sky-blue that brought out the colour of her eyes. With strappy beige sandals on her feet and pretty gold drops in her ears, Lila planned to knock Josh off his feet.

She giggled at herself suddenly in the mirror as she paced. *You dope*, she thought. *All this and it's not even a first date.*

They'd gone out a lot in the weeks that they'd been together, but tonight felt different. Somehow.

Her heart sped up as she heard the doorbell.

"I'll get it!" she shouted hastily, smoothing down her dress and giving herself one last assessing gaze in her bedroom mirror.

Lila slowed halfway down her headlong descent of the stairs with a sudden anxious vision of Josh opening the door to find her sprawled in a fallen heap on the carpet. Definitely *not* the impression she wanted to give. Smoothing her dress down with trembling hands and pressing her lips together one last time to fix her gloss in place, she opened the door.

"Hi," she said, feeling ridiculously shy.

Josh visibly shook his head, like a dog with water in its ears. "Um, hi," he said. He sounded a little dazed. "Wow, Lila, you look . . . amazing."

Lila's tummy squirmed with pleasure. "Thanks. You look pretty good too," she said. "No sketchbook?"

"Not tonight," he said.

Lila stroked the lapels of his jacket. "I like the suit."

Josh looked down at his suit with an air of surprise. "What, this old thing?"

Reaching up around his neck, Lila yanked off a price tag poking up from the inside of the jacket.

"Dang, I'm smooth," he said a little ruefully.

Lila laughed. *You're perfect*, she thought.

He was holding a bunch of white roses in his hand. Lila felt warm as she looked at the flowers' dark green foliage and tightly furled petals. Flowers were predictable, maybe, but that didn't make it a bad thing. Right now, it was the loveliest thing in the world.

"Are those for me?" she said.

Josh peered behind her into the hall. "I was thinking of giving them to your cat, actually."

Lila giggled. "We don't have a cat."

Josh stared at the number on the door. "Do I have the wrong house?"

Reaching over the threshold, she drew him into the hallway. "You don't have the wrong house and the flowers are gorgeous. I'll put them in some water. The cat will love them, just as soon as I can persuade Mum to get one."

Josh smiled at her and Lila's heart took wings. She wanted to kiss him right now, but something stopped her. Maybe it was the fact that her mother was lurking on the landing up the stairs, doing her best to look unobtrusive. She dragged Josh into the kitchen instead.

"I have some news," Josh said, leaning against the side as she filled a vase with water and arranged the roses. "You remember Dorothy Watkins?"

Lila had to think for a minute. "As in Dorothy Watkins, Andrew the cat and the atlas?" she said curiously.

"I sent the story you wrote to a magazine." He grinned at her. "They loved it."

Lila could only stare. *What* had he just said?

"You sent it to a magazine?" she managed. "The story I scribbled down in about ten minutes at the station for your illustrations?"

"It was good. I typed it up. Emailed it across to them last week. They're going to publish it."

He didn't seem to realize that there were volcanoes

suddenly exploding in Lila's head. She laughed out loud in pure shock. "Josh, are you *serious*?"

He looked a little worried. "You don't mind, do you?"

She sat down very suddenly on a kitchen chair. Falling down in a dead faint in front of your date was not good. "Mind?" she said. "Josh, you. . . I. . ."

Launching herself from the chair, she hit her target square-on, wrapping her arms and legs tightly around Josh's entire body so that he almost fell backwards into the sink.

"Thank you," she squealed against his neck. "Thank you, thank you, thank you."

"Do I take it that you're pleased?" he said into her ear.

Lila was having difficulty keeping her tears in check. "I'm absolutely furious," she said, holding him even tighter. "And I'm never going to talk to you again."

"I knew I should have given those flowers to the cat."

They stayed like that for a few minutes, before he set her gently down on the floor again. "We have a date," he said. "Things to do and places to go. Remember?"

Lila was having trouble remembering even her name. She gripped Josh's hand and nodded while her heart sang like a bird. At long, long last, she had a glimmer of what her future might hold. She'd have to work at it, but maybe her idle daydream of being a writer one day wasn't so crazy. She finally felt like she had something to look forward to. It was the most precious thing Josh could have given her.

TWENTY-ONE

"So where are we going?" Lila asked, letting Josh lead her out into the evening and down the road. "A restaurant, the cinema, where?"

"I thought we could go to the pier."

Lila felt the tiniest hint of disappointment. She'd hoped for something a bit more original than the pier. They *always* went to the pier.

Josh is doing his best, she reminded herself. *And he did send your story to a magazine, and bring you flowers*. "Perfect," she said bravely.

He was walking a little faster now, pulling her along by the hand. Lila did her best to keep up. She was glad now that she had decided to wear sandals. She could kick them off if Josh wanted to go to their usual place on the sand. It didn't matter where they went really, because she was with Josh and that was all that mattered.

The beach was busy, still warm and full of people enjoying themselves. To Lila's surprise, instead of leading her down to the right of the pier and on to the sand, Josh pulled her on past the pier entrance and down to the marina.

"Where are we going?" said Lila, glancing back at the pier in confusion.

Josh strode down one of the jetties, stopping beside a beautiful speedboat made of polished wood, with cream-coloured leather seats and a large chrome-plated wheel. A jaunty blue-and-white flag fluttered at the stern as he jumped aboard.

Lila looked around, suddenly worried that the boat owner would come striding down the jetty shouting at them. "Josh, I don't think you're allowed on there," she said.

Josh looked amused. "Then I'll call the harbour master and complain. It's ours. For tonight, anyway."

Lila wondered how many fresh surprises she could take this evening. She stared at the polished wood and chrome, the expensive-looking dashboard and the little fluttering flag. It must have cost a *fortune*.

"I sold all the gear Mum bought for me and hired it," he said, noticing her expression as he helped her aboard. The boat rocked gently under her feet. "I'd much rather cruise around Heartside Bay with you. And don't worry, I know how to drive a boat. Grandpa's taken me out fishing lots of times."

Lila sank down on an expensive cream leather sofa. Heartside Bay looked completely different from the water. "I can't believe you've done this," she said. "You don't *do* surprises like this."

Josh cast off and started up the engine. "Looks like I'll have to convince you," he said as he steered out into the bay. "Where do you want to go?"

This really is happening, she thought. She stretched out luxuriously on the leather seat, wiggling her toes in the warm air. "Just drive," she said in the lordliest tone she could manage.

Josh laughed. "As you wish, my lady."

They cruised along the coast, watching the seals basking on the rocks and the surfers at play, counting the sails that they saw and trying to come up with ways of describing shapes the gulls were making as they wheeled through the sky. Gull shapes were harder to define than clouds because they moved so quickly. They admired the way the sun gilded the cliffs as it sank closer to the sea. It wasn't hard to imagine sailing right into the sun, Lila thought. There was a story in there somewhere.

"Sail me to the Caribbean," Lila instructed lazily as the sun finally began to dip beyond the horizon, lying back on the leather seats and shading her eyes from the buttery sunlight.

"I have a better idea."

Feeling the ground bump beneath the boat, Lila sat up in surprise and stared at the stretch of rocks and sand before her. Then she felt a delicious stab of recognition.

"Kissing Island!" she gasped. Jumping out of the boat, she spun around, taking in the familiar shape of the little outcropping with the curve of the main town beach a short distance to the north.

"I couldn't arrange the tides in our favour tonight," Josh said, catching her around the waist.

Lila put her arms laughingly around his neck. "I should fire you for that. Your résumé clearly stated that you could control the wind and the water."

"Do you remember when I first brought you here?" he asked, stroking her face with the back of his hand.

As if she could forget! Crossing the causeway hand in hand with Josh had been the most romantic experience of Lila's life. The moonlight, the clock tower chiming midnight way off across the water. . . *If you kiss your love on Kissing Island at midnight of a full moon, you will be together for ever. . .*

"I remember," she said.

His eyes were bright with affection. "It all started here, didn't it?"

"It started when I trod on your toe outside history," Lila corrected. "It's just that you didn't get around to kissing me for a while after that."

"I've wasted so much time," he said. "I don't want to waste any more."

As he kissed her, Lila tasted the sea spray on his lips. The tide could have come in and washed the whole of Kissing Island away and she wouldn't have noticed.

When the kiss finally ended, she rested her head on his jacket, content just to be.

"We're going to be late," he said into her hair.

"Oh!" Lila gasped as Josh suddenly lifted her off the sand and carried her back to the boat.

Within moments, the engine was running and their boat was carving a wide arc away from the island and back towards the shore. Lila had wanted Josh to mix things up a little, but she'd been enjoying their interlude on Kissing Island. How many surprises did he want to fit into the evening? Where were they going now?

Josh brought the boat along the shore, rounding the cliff point by the secret cove. Lila registered people on the silver cove sands, running beside the water and waving.

"It's Rhi!" she said in astonishment, sitting up in the stern. "And Brody. And Eve, and Becca, and. . . Josh, what's going on?"

"Your last party was a wash-out," Josh replied as he brought the boat bumping gently into shore. "I thought we should have another one."

Lila found herself surrounded by her friends, all reaching into the boat to help her out, laughing and joking, admiring her dress and making envious noises about the boat.

"Your face," Polly giggled as she pulled Lila up on to the sand. "Didn't Josh say anything?"

Josh was laughing with Brody and Ollie, who had both climbed into the boat. He glanced Lila's way, winked and blew her a kiss.

"He didn't say a word!" Lila declared, marvelling.

"He's not an international man of mystery for nothing," said Eve. "I helped organize it, of course. We thought we'd surprise you."

"You've certainly done that."

"It's a party for Polly and Ollie too," Rhi put in. "Our last chance to be together before they jet off to San Francisco next week."

"I take it that you and Josh are back together?" Eve asked. "Just so I'm clear?"

Lila nodded. "And it's even better than before," she said shyly.

"Of course it is," announced Polly with a heartfelt sigh. "It's true love. Kissing Island never lies."

Lila gazed around at the beach, the people and the noise and the atmosphere. The rugs on the warm sand, the campfire and the barbecue and the rock pools filled with chilling bottles of soda. *This* was a party. Iris, Leo, Flynn – they didn't have a clue.

"What do you think?" said Josh, pushing through the crowd towards her.

She shook her head wordlessly.

"Nothing to say?" he teased, putting his arms around her. "That's a first."

Lila found her voice.

"Kiss me, Josh," she said.

"Whatever you say, my lady."

LOOK OUT FOR MORE

HEARTSIDE BAY

Life, love and everything in between
HEARTSIDE BAY
The New Girl
CATHY COLE

Life, love and everything in between
HEARTSIDE BAY
The Trouble With Love
CATHY COLE

Life, love and everything in between
HEARTSIDE BAY
A Date With Fate
CATHY COLE
Life, love and everything in between
HEARTSIDE BAY
More Than a Love Song
CATHY COLE

Life, love and everything in between
HEARTSIDE BAY
Never a Perfect Moment
CATHY COLE

Life, love and everything in between
HEARTSIDE BAY
Kiss at Midnight
CATHY COLE

Life, love and everything in between
HEARTSIDE BAY
Back to You
CATHY COLE

Life, love and everything in between
HEARTSIDE BAY
Summer of Secrets
CATHY COLE